# My Dear Reflection

### Jane Jamila Nakasamu

WESTBOW
PRESS®
A DIVISION OF THOMAS NELSON
& ZONDERVAN

WestBow Press books may be ordered through booksellers or by contacting:

WestBow Press
A Division of Thomas Nelson & Zondervan
1663 Liberty Drive
Bloomington, IN 47403
www.westbowpress.com
1 (866) 928-1240

ISBN: 978-1-5127-1918-5 (sc)

Library of Congress Control Number: 2015918674

Print information available on the last page.

WestBow Press rev. date: 11/09/2015

My Dear Reflection,

Life is not a book, it's not a cooked up illusion or creamed fantasy…its reality. When I stare into the mirror I see my reflection, more than that I see you, My Dear Reflection and it makes me reflect on the past, how all this started. People ask me so many questions that I fail to answer, truth is I have never had the courage to, but now I do.

I am telling the world our story and I accept whatever consequences come with it, for now I am ready, the only question is; are you ready to hear it?

# Contents

# Preface

This book is one of its kind, a collection in the Smile Productions aimed at telling untold stories from the heart of Africa. It is the first edition of My Dear Reflection.

Growing up in ghetto in Zambia is not easy, too many circumstances stand in the way of those who want to rise above the tide. Join the wonderful identical twins with different personalities and strengths but they share a common passion and drive which enables them to rise above every tide in their lives.

In the story, Emmy is born with a sickness that limits her abilities, she struggles through school and separates herself from society. She is very vulnerable and feels abnormal but learns that she should not limited by her weaknesses. Emily is able-bodied and brilliant but she takes on more than she can handle and this leads to disastrous consequences.

The book takes the reader deep into the characters thoughts, feelings that are expressed with passion through poetry allowing the reader to feel every emotion felt.

# Acknowledgement

My sincere thanks are due to the following individuals and organisations.

Charles and Chewaga Nakasamu, my dear parents, for cheering me on during my author's journey and providing inspiration for my books.

Andrea Ferrario and Rudia M Ferrario for providing funding for publishing and moral support.

Annie Ngoma, Mutinta Nakasamu, Sydney Mareya, Dennis Simainga, Simutelo Nakasamu, Mzie Moyo, Jacob Moji and Semba Kamuliwo for their support and help with editing and reviewing the book.

WestBow press for publishing services. Lulu.com for providing guidance and knowledge on book publishing.

I would like to acknowledge the input of all these individuals and organisations during the writing and publishing stages. I would also like to highlight that the events of this book are not historically accurate and most events are based on fiction.

Thank you.

*In Memory of Abdul Mohammed.*

I stared at my reflection as if in a mirror…I was confused as to whether it was me or someone else. Eyes blood stained, swollen in pain with veins pumping blood to the heart that was failing and a body that was dying, I watched as the tears washed away all that was left of me, was I beholding myself, was it my dear reflection?

# Introduction

It was not perfect but it was fine, so much better than what he started with, despite his amazing skills and great talent Chewe Lengwe never went to University, no he never had the money to, he worked at a car repair auto shop and he didn't make much there, something had to be done, he knew it himself. Chewe saved up till he could pay for a course at a college not so far from where he stayed, so that he could keep working, there he met and fell in love with Priscilla, he so much wanted to be marry her, no doubt she was the one; she was beautiful, kind and a very decent girl with a strong personality, but she too was struggling in fact she had to drop out of school because her family could no longer afford it, he had no money to marry her either so he worked and worked and worked.

Mr Lengwe waddled around his face very sweaty, it had been a long day of work under the scorching Zambian sun, his work attire had oils stains, and he was so drained. He was now at the hospital waiting to see what his wife had for him, the air here was different and it smelt like medicine, in his mind he imagined how he would drive his son to work showing him all the manly things he did at his new job, he even imagined-his fantasy was cut short when a nurse came looking for him, he took off his hat in amazement when he discovered that he had not one but two, girls?

They were the most adorable babies to look at; Emmy had beautiful big brown eyes and thick dark curly hair with a straight face whilst Emily had a round chubby face, thick rosy pink lips and a beautiful shimmering deep caramel complexion.

Their parents were so happy to have two beautiful twins and they did all they could to provide for them but times were hard and the economy was building more problems. Only three months after birth, Emmy fell ill and when her parents took her to the hospital they discovered that she had a rare case of diabetes, the treatment was expensive and even when they had sold all they could to treat her, her condition improved only a little. They had to move to a cheaper neighbourhood that was not very nice and in order for Emmy to be healthy they spent so much money, her illness made her vulnerable.

Emmy grew up in awe to her parents for all the sacrifices they made for her but Emily felt like Emmy got all the attention. They started school together; in fact Emily had to wait for Emmy to get a little more stable in order for them to start school together at a nearby basic school. Emily was a fast learner and she had a photographic memory whilst Emmy was a slow learner and because she often fell ill she lagged behind but she was always determined to catch up.

# Chapter 1

## *Twin berries aren't the same*

He strolled across the classroom; it was old, very old, and so old that it lost all its layers of paint and it looked like an old tree. The room was big and fully occupied, he exercised himself as he walked around with chalk stains all over his beige jacket. His eyes glanced around the classroom and most of the pupils began to sink in their chairs, suddenly he posed and pointed at the shy girl who sat at the back-corner of the classroom.

"You!" He said whilst pointing at Emmy.

"Me?" she responded with uncertainty.

"Yes you…who else am I pointing at, what is the capital city of Tunisia?"

"Hmm, the capital city of Tunisia is…Accra?" she responded doubtingly.

"No it's not. Accra, class what is the capital city of Tunisia?" the teacher asked again. The class was silent, it was so silent that silence itself was making noise.

"Huh," the teacher sighed in shock realising that he had just spent thirty minutes talking to egg shells, his face lit up as he said "Emily, what is the correct answer?" with hope that the class had hope.

"You saying it…just lose the a-a" Emily said facing a window whilst she chewed gum very frustrated as she usually was in class; she tried so many times to convince her parents that school was too boring and she could just read everything from books.

"Just answer…" the teacher insisted.

"Tunis… Tunis," Emily responded with frustration.

Then one boy in the class giggled and said in vernacular, "It's so funny, they look so alike but one of them has the brain of a chicken." Making the once so silent class burst into thunderous laughter, Emmy got so sad that she began to cry in class; her sister then comforted her. On their way home as they walked home they met a group of boys one of which had previously provoked Emmy in class.

"Hey Bro, these are the twins I was talking about…." He told his friends in vernacular.

"Sis, there is the ugly looking one I was telling you about," Emily told her twin sister very loudly in vernacular. Then the boy's friends started laughing at him and he got so upset that he followed Emily and pushed her saying she shouldn't mess with him. Then Emily got angry and slapped him making his dark chubby face darker and chubbier, the boy then got more aggressive and began to argue with Emily, Emmy on the other hand got in the middle trying to stop them unfortunately her blood pressure rose and she fainted. The boys got so afraid that they ran away, Emily was able to get help and take her sister home. When they got home their mom was so worried and began to take care of her.

"Emily, don't just sleep there fetch me water for your sister." Her mother, Mrs Lengwe, said to her.

"Uhhh, mum, I'm injured too." Emily told her whilst she dragged herself off the bed.

"Can't you see your sister is unconscious!" her mother yelled.

Half an hour later, Emmy woke up and was very weak, when she was awake Emily went to sleep again. Her father, Mr Lengwe, came back from work; he was working for ZESCO the national electricity company as a mechanic. He immediately went to see Emmy and sat next to her asking how she was feeling, Emmy said she was weak and Mr Lengwe told Emily to prepare something for Emmy to eat.

"What?? I just got on the bed." Emily said in frustration.

"Hey, don't argue with your dad, just go." Her mother told her.

"I'm injured too, that boy hit me, not Emmy, she just panicked and fainted!" Emily said trying to justify herself.

"Oh, so you were fighting again…this is your fault Emily, we don't have money to start rushing her to the hospital if she gets worse." Her mother told her.

"No, it's not my fault she is a sickling, I don't want to be her babysitter!" Emily said as she stormed out of the house.

"Let her go, we will deal with her later." Mr Lengwe told Mrs Lengwe who wanted to follow her so that she could discipline her the African way.

Emily ran outside, she was so angry.

'Am I invisible, I am so dark that they cannot see me? All they see is Emmy, Emmy, Emmy
Emmy this, Emmy that, Emmy is the enemy that makes Emily look guilty.
It's not fair, I have to do everything and she just lies around because she is sick,
Well I'm sick too, sick and tired of all this running around for Emmy.
Nobody cares about me, well, neither do I'

The neighbourhood they lived in was densely populated so even though it was night there were so many young people moving about. As she was running she ran past the boy who she had a previous encounter with.

"Aaah, there is that arrogant girl," said the boy who got into a fight with Emily. He then followed her behind and grabbed her. He took her to the rest of the crew,

"Look, here she is, what should we do to her?" he asked.

"let's beat her," one of the boy's said.

"We can't beat a girl" another argued.

"ahh, this one is not a girl, she's rough" said the boy who fought with her.

"Wait" the ringleader said, "she looks sad," he then approached her

"young girl, what's your name?" he asked. She simply rolled her eyes at him, "my name is Dwain...why are you sad?" he continued.

Emily looked down and said, "I'm not sad, I am angry, stay away from me." Emily said pushing him back.

Dwain laughed and was fascinated, he told the rest of the crew to leave them alone as he talked to her.

"We are alone now, I know your just afraid, what's your name?"

"Emily..."she told him, "and I'm sad because, nobody pays attention to me."

"You don't need attention, what you need is a warm cup of tea..." he said as he wrapped her a cigarette. She was resistant at first but when she smoked a little, she couldn't let go.

"Heey, take it easy" he told her, she was holding the cigarette tightly with her lips and sucked the life out of it until she chocked and started coughing. Her eyes were watery and red, her face still swollen from her encounter with her classmate; Dwain carefully watched her every move and he grew fond of her. He could tell that she had a bad day, he was slightly tall and had curly hair, his skin was golden brown and he had piercing brown eyes; it was easy to tell from his appearance that his family was of mixed race blood but he never got to know his family for he was an orphan abandoned by his mother in the streets at an early age and even though he was raised in an orphanage, he made the street his home. Dwain identified loneliness in Emily, he could see it in her eyes; something that none of his friends could understand. He pated Emily on her back and told her to go home and sleep before she got into more trouble, she immediately turned from him and he watched her leave as she walked away she looked back at him with a different expression that said she was glad she met him and he could read that.

"Tomorrow I can make you cocoa," he said to her and she smiled back at him.

Emily sneaked into her bedroom through her window and went straight into her blankets. She had a smile on her face, Emmy was woken up by the strange smell that was diluted by the air in the room, she know that Emily had been smoking but she did not want to tell her parents because she feared the trouble she would put her sister in so she approached her sister, she had a long grey gown on and a cotton jersey, her face was pale and her eyes bigger than ever, she stood in front of her sisters bed and began to poke her,

"Emmm, Emmmm" she whispered silently, she then poked even harder until Emily rose out of her blankets with a strange smile on her face.

"Where were you?" Emmy asked

"Not here…" Emily responded

"Who were you with?"

"Not you…"

"What were you doing?" Emmy asked again, then Emily paused for a second and smiled "not smoking," as she fell back on the bed. Emily tried to wake her up but she had fallen into a deep sleep. She sat on her bed for a while, she knew that this was the beginning of something bad in her sister's life and she knew it was all because of her. Emmy felt her heart ache, she wished she had been normal that way her sister would not be burdened by herself, she pitied herself but even more she pitied her lovely twin sister and what would become of her.

How could I explain what I could not understand?
How could I understand what I had not experienced how
could I experience what I have never known,
I want to be the one to pull her out of her cage but;
I am the one who put her there in the first place,
Oh sister, that I had been more like you and less like me, then we would be perfect pair
Sown together by destiny's ties but our bond is merely a coincidence,
You are you, I am me but we are not we.

# Chapter 2

## *Girl meets world*

The weather was unfriendly, it was mid-June and everyone in the classroom was covered from head to toe with what appeared to be a mass assembly of winter jerseys. The sky was gloomy grey and the streets were empty, everyone took shelter except for the unlucky students who were at school. The teachers made their lessons short as if shortening the lessons would make time speed up but in the end, the students were left with extra time to stay in school till it was time to knock off. It was cold and some of the girls began to go home; the poor eighth grade girls could hardly bare the weather so they jumped out of windows in order to run away from school. If only the governments could make the cold season a holiday but alas, the economy could not bear any more holidays; they needed people working and students learning.

Emmy wrapped herself in a little blanket and her body was curved in to keep her warm, she was too distracted by the science book she was reading to leave the classroom before it was actually time up. Her eyes quickly moved across the book as she was fascinated by the contents of the book, they dilated and shone bright brown under the rays of little sunlight that penetrated the clouds and shot across the windows into the classroom. Who knew all the vitamins that could be found in a little strawberry she thought to herself, she went on reading and her mouth was wide open as she flipped the page to the next chapter but the page could not flip; it was held down by what seemed to be a piece of chalk alas…it was Emily's finger that was so pale it looked white.

"Let's go home" said the figure blocking the light from reaching her book.

"It's not yet time, the guard won't let us through." Emmy told her

"We'll use the back fence" Emily responded trying to persuade her.

"that's illegal, it's almost time up." Emmy said when really the only reason that she was staying was because she wanted to finish her book. Emily simply shrugged her shoulders and went back to her sit, there she lay back and lit up a cigarette to keep herself warm. Her sister was too attached to her book to notice the deviant act of her twin sister.

They walked down the cold road together, Emily was looking really pale and even caught a flu; it was as if she was the one suffering from an illness when really it was her sister. She had not been taking care of herself because she spent too much time with the gang she was affiliated to and was barely at home except when her parents came back from work, but they came back really late. Her father worked late at an electricity company and her mother even later at a supermarket as a teller. When her father was done working he would drive to the supermarket and wait for her mother to knock off then they would both go home. That gave Emily enough time to be with her gang; she would barely eat or study she would just move around with them, play soccer and video games; in spite of her playfulness she would always come first in class, all she would do was read Emmy's neatly written notes when their parents were back from work and never see a book again. It was a bargain for Emily, her good grades would justify her every act and Emmy was not bold enough to tell her parents what she was really up to.

When they got home Emily quickly fried some kapenta (small dried fish), made a quick lunch for her and her sister then off she was into the hood knowing Emmy would take care of the rest. She ran to the football ground and even before she got in the pitch she threw her skirt and jersey on a wire remaining with some shorts and started to play soccer. She was not necessarily skilled, she just enjoyed the thrill of the game and made a good defender because of her aggression.

It was three minutes to game over and there was anxiety in the atmosphere. All the players were worn out and sweated like it was summer day. Dust was rising and so were tempers, the mid fielders of one team were stealing the ball and they dribbled it till it reached dangerous areas, one of the defenders was Emily the tiger herself, she guarded the ball like a cub and made sure it did not leave her sight. One of the players tried to make a long shot but Emily blocked it with her chest, it was time up but the player claimed she committed a foul by using her hand, Emily defended herself but soon it turned into a fight because the boy was telling her that she was a girl and should be cooking lunch at home. Emily was angry, this was not the first time she was mocked or treated unfairly just because she was a girl. She liked spending time with Dwain and the crew because there it did not matter what she looked like, she could act spontaneous and did not have to worry about expressing herself however she felt. Girls of her age were made to stay at home cooking and cleaning whilst boys only had a few chores and they were free to go wherever they liked, she did not like to be locked up in one place, she did not like to be told how to think, feel or act; she wanted to be free to see things for herself and experience life without being told where she did or did not belong. In fact, sometimes she dressed up as a boy so that she could not be judged when she was hanging around with the crew, society made it difficult for her to express herself but Emily was a like a wild tiger that was not to be tamed.

Who says what? Let me see you,
and give you an education in individual expression,
I am who am and I will be what I will,
Judge I don't care, it don't matter.
Just because I wear skirt doesn't make me weak,
I will achieve what I seek, in fact I know I'm so much smarter than all you female
haters…I am free like bird swift as an eagle but don't mess with me, I'm a tigress,
Can be careless be warned,
I can't be tamed, and I'm naturally adorned with this vigour charisma,
see me as I become a professional football star….for Man U!

After the game they went to the orphanage to help Dwain with his chores so that they could spend the rest afternoon playing video games at the orphanage. When they were done playing video games Dwain sneaked out of the orphanage to join his friend who were waiting outside the premises, it was time for a service at the chapel and all the orphans were required to attend but Dwain usually sneaked out, he pretended to see his friends off and smiled at the nuns who were heading to the hall; the nuns liked him because he was very friendly to all the orphans and took care of the little ones but they did not know what he did in his spare time; after the nuns entered the hall, he ran to the bathrooms and used the window to sneak out and jump over the wall. When he met his friends outside they all ran really fast till they were out of the covenant radius. They ran till they were far from the ghetto, they jumped over some pipes and made their way across the railway to a little hill which they climbed until the top, there was a big old tree with giant leaves and thick branches which they also climbed. When they reached the top they sat on one of its branches next to each other, Thomas followed by Chims, then Hazwa; the one who bullied Emily when she was younger, Emily herself and lastly Dwain the leader of the gang. Dwain was very gentle and kind, he was a good boy with misdirected motives. He knew how to take care of others but never really did take care of himself, he was a bright boy especially when he was younger; he dreamt of being the President but he lost all his motivation when he began to realise that he was abandoned by his mother when he was young then all his potential was lost, he began to use drugs but the only thing he had not lost was his kind heart. He began to hand his friends bottles of beer that were hidden in a hole in the trunk of the giant tree, he handed Emily a cigarette; she never drank alcohol, she just smoked with them. Then on that hill, they watched the sun set into the city of Lusaka together, they did that almost every day but today something was different;

"Hey, what's up?" Emily asked Dwain who gave a sad smile, he looked at the sunset and looked back at her.

"As time goes by, I will soon approach my 18ᵗʰ year." Dwain said,

"So???" Emily asked,

"So….Dwain will be chased from the orphanage, he's too old" Hazwa said.

"Huh, where will you go?" Emily asked Dwain, her expression deepened as she took a deep breath of her cigarette and slowly blew the smoke into the azure sky,

"I don't know, I messed up my life." Dwain told her.

"Ahh, come on, you'll figure it out, you are Dj D…." Emily assured her friend but Dwain gave a heartfelt smile and tried to believe her words.

Emily could tell that Dwain was worried and she could not stand seeing him worried so she stood and walked toward the trunk of the tree, there she engraved the letters D for Dwain and E for Emily with O and P in between and said, "wherever you go just know I am somewhere in Lusaka, doping because I remembered you." Dwain could not find comfort in her words; he knew he had dragged her into his dark cave that proved to be his damnation.

"But Emily, you are brilliant, try pay some attention to school." Dwain said,

"Uhh, yeah…. you know I should, try be like Emmy…" she said then Hazwa shared a stare with her for a second then Emily and Hazwa burst into laughter.

If only she knew, if only she saw what life really looks like maybe she could grow
I treasured her like my younger sister and kept her close to me but
only to be destroyed because I wanted to be happy.
I cherished her and spoiled her with things that would damage
her treating her as the only family I have.
I have been selfish and led her to this path I thought was my comfort zone.
Her lovely brown eyes and tender golden skin, I watch it shimmer in the
twilight I watch her as she puffs up smoke and I know I have killed her.
If I had let her to cry the tears of her childhood, if I had ignored her gaze
then maybe she would be in a better place with better people looking smart
and beautiful girl, because that what she truly is; not like a dirty boy in a
place called kabwata but like a gem living in the luxuries kabulonga.

But how could I, when I felt her pain and remembered my sorrowful years, the years I had a conscious and a heart, when I could feel deep neglect and tormenting loneliness. How could I let her walk by and see her cry, How could I…

"Hey, what's on your mind?" Emily asked Dwain who was blankly staring at her,

"The only thing left in my brain."

# Chapter 3

## *Mirror Mirror*

Emily got back home she found her sister staring deeply into a mirror. "Stare all you want, it won't look nicer..." Emily said teasing her.

"You know we are identical right???" Emmy responded cutting her sisters joke, her sister then gave an ashamed expression and left the room to take a quick bath before she could go to the table to study. Emily was not staring at the mirror to see how she looked but she was actually studying her eyes. She was so passionate about Science and applied it to almost everything in her life, it was the only way she could actually remember and soon she discovered that it could be a studying tactic.

Emily discovered the world of books and she was often reading so many books, she could easily hide herself in the secret world of literature and biology but it upset her that no matter how much she read, her sister would always be better than her so she read even more and soon it became a passion, she could not go a day without reading a novel the same way her sister could not go a day without smoking a cigarette.

Time went by like a passing wind and soon they were in their ninth grade about to write their exams. Emmy spent most of her time at the school library whilst Emily would pretend to be at the library with Emily but really she was with the gang.

She tried to read the text but all she could see was a thick cloud, then with resentment she put on her spectacles and continued reading. She was angry that also her eyes were failing her, she did now know what it would be next...her hands maybe. She was solving some equations but they proved too difficult. The librarian couldn't help but notice her struggle, she was also making a disturbing sound each time she found a wrong answer so she walked up to her and said. "Can I help?"

"No thanks" Emmy said, realising she was making noise.

"Hey, I wrote my exams a year ago, do you want to go through the paper with me?" This time the librarian used a better strategy that Emmy could not resist, she simply nodded.

Emmy did not have too many friends because most people were afraid that they would upset her and make her sick so she was not so used to making new friends but she could tell the Librarian genuinely wanted to help her so she let her do so, it was quite productive except for a few questions that they could not answer.

"You know what, my elder brother is really good at math and he teaches me so let me call him so that…" before she could finish her sentence, Emmy dashed out saying it was time for her to go and cook supper at home. The librarian was left standing; she then looked behind and whispered, "I tried" to a young man who sat on a table behind her studying Biology.

Emmy arrived at home and put a pot of water to boil on the pot then she went outside to pluck some vegetables but was surprised to find Emily's friend outside.

"Dwain, what are you doing here?" she asked him trying to normalize the situation.

"Hi, I wanted to talk to you." He said, there was something off about him, in spite the new clothes he was wearing.

"I am no longer staying at the orphanage, I will be moving in with a friend to a new town, Kabwe but I don't think I will stay long there either." Emmy bended towards him as she paid more attention, she had never talked to him, "so I wanted to say, you and E might not be so alike but you are her reflection and she is yours so….as in, just take care of her, let her not lose it completely." He said making her feel bad.

"You know how stubborn she is." Emmy told him

"I know but I care a lot and she does care about you so much, so promise me when mum and dad find out about her, you'll have her back?" he asked her to pledge

"I can't promise that" Emmy said as her emotions arose,

"Ok promise me you will always look out for her?" He said,

"Ok….I'll try my best" Emmy said, she could not disappoint Dwain, she didn't have to but he had a way of connecting with people and it was working with her.

After saying that, he left walking towards the wire fence and waving before he left the yard, she could tell that he was afraid of what was to happen next. Only a few minutes later, Emily came running into the house and into the bedroom banging the door behind her, Emmy knew she was sad and she was crying but Emily did not like exposing her emotions so she played music in the room really loud whilst she cried, Emmy could still hear her cry through all the music and she was heartbroken, she empathised with her as she cooked the food, she know Dwain was a good friend of hers and his departure left Emily really lonely, she felt like going to comfort her but she did not know how to, her helplessness left her feeling very depressed and at that moment she remembered Dwain's words about their relationship, she could not control the tear from her own eye.

Ten minutes later she could still hear her sister crying in their bed room, Emmy put reason aside and stormed into the bedroom where her sister was on the bed crying, Emily suddenly stopped crying and hesitated while she was planning on how to send her sister out but Emmy climbed onto the bed next to her and picked up a piece of mirror that she from a side table, she lifted it up to her sisters face and showed her the round swollen looking face that was being reflected,

"Emily, if the mirror keeps reflecting this…just know I will always be here for you." Then she grabbed her sister and hugged her so tightly, Emily couldn't resist her, she had no strength to push her away; she needed her sister when she lost a friend.

That night Emily did not pretend to study but she went to sleep early, when their parents were back from work Emmy told them that she was not feeling well. She wanted her sister to have some privacy so she spent the night studying and when it was really late she went outside to sit by the veranda. It was late October and the weather was quite hot, the moon shone brightly and all the stars decorated the Sky like a garden of diamonds. Emmy felt different; she was used to always being weak, always being emotional and always being sick but today, she felt stronger and she saw that she had the ability to help someone.

"I want to help people," she said silently, "who cannot help themselves, I want to help people who are like me… weak and sick,…but how can I?" she asked,

"By doing what you do best" replied a voice from behind, then Emmy turned startled, she looked back.

"Emmy, you don't have to be strong to help someone, you just need to use what you have. Me and your mum don't have much, we don't make so much money but that shouldn't stop us from helping other relatives who are suffering like we are. Ok?"

"Yes Dad."

The silence during that moment was golden as Emmy reflected on the words of her Father who had been outside fixing his car, maybe she was not so helpless after all, maybe she did not have to lock herself up in the world of Love Novels and Science text books, maybe other people would look at her differently if she looked at herself differently, maybe she could actually do more than she always thought she could. The future was looking brighter, it was as if one of the stars in the sky had granted her wish Emmy felt optimistic; meanwhile; Emily could not sleep, she was troubled by so many thoughts that stole sleep from her; she couldn't imagine life without her friend who she grew up with, who was always there when she needed someone, who was now gone to a place even he did not know.

I wish to feel nothing, but I feel everything;
From love to hate…pain to gain, my heart has exploded with all the
emotion it can possibly express. That I would isolate my being to
an abyss free from feeling, I would pay a handsome price.
That I could brush it all aside and leave my life but it won't leave me alone. It being
anger, doubt within and without, even if I scream and shout there is no way out.
That I could be reincarnated into a second existence with no
remembrance of the former, be my guest of honour.
So I sat in the cold across and open window and stared at the sky filled
with stars and saw how lonely I was…if isolated. I am alone, right?

The next morning Emmy got up early and made her sister something to eat but her sister left without a word ignoring her courtesy, Emily's face was pink and her eyes swollen, she covered it with a scarf and avoided any eye contact. Emmy promised herself that she would not let her sister's anger spoil her good mood, she was off to face the world with and wide smile. When she got to school she no longer rushed through the corridors trying to avoid meeting people but she lifted her head high in honest confidence; in fact, most people mistook her for her sister who was also mistaken for Emmy since she was so low and silent. It was a strange day for the twins but Emmy embraced it! She had a new world view; why, she felt like she could carry the world on her shoulder whilst Emily was feeling like the weight of the world was on her back.

The teacher strolled across the class, most of the girls were biting their lips and scratching their hair trying to figure out the answer to the question that was just asked. At the back corner of the class was a hand that was not quite sure about its position; the girl was debating with herself…she seemed to want to talk but pulled herself back. 'Should I, no…there's no need, but I have to, ok, I'll do it, but I can't why…' the teacher noticed her struggle and was worried if she was not feeling well, then suddenly she stood up and shouted "Constitution!" abruptly taking everyone's attention. The teacher was shocked, he paused for a second and did not really know what to say, and then he said. "No, that's not correct but thanks for the courage!" Emmy remained standing, she did not know what just happened, adrenaline rushed so quickly to her head and she froze, then slowly she lowered herself till she finally sat down and landed on her wooden desk; half eaten by rats.

It was a break-through in her life, one that she would live to remember; this did not make her any less afraid or thoughtless but it was a step closer to courage. That afternoon she went to the library and when she got there she looked for the librarian she had met previously, Emmy scarcely made friends so she was looking for the right words to say but it was too late when the librarian popped up in front of her, "Hey you" she exclaimed with a slight jump, "Hi" Emmy replied hesitantly in a high pitched voice, then the librarian remained looking at her curiously with her head shaking from side to side slowly. She was tall and slim, her skin a warm umber, her hair was short and curly with a fine mosh texture, she wore specs but you could still see her beautiful dark eyes through them,…Emmy realised she had to say something, "I am, mm, you really helped me with math." She said then she posed and scorned herself in her mind.

"Anytime, my name is Mpange." She said with a friendly smile,

"Emmy then smiled back at her and said, "I am Emmy."

She also made a friend that day, it was a day she would remember because Mpange not only helped her with her school work but supported her both psychologically and emotionally.

There was a figure, curled up in a dark corner besides an abandoned workshop shivering and coughing surrounded by a group of boys, they seemed to know the person in fact they were consoling the person; then they handed the person a tissue, with some white ash in it, the shadow of someone desperately needing a friend hit the wall illuminated by a small bulb from across the street; it pulled out its shaking hand to first wipe its face and then get the tissue and brought it close to its face.

## Chapter 4

### *How did I get here?*

Screams filled the corridors as girls were going to the deputy headmistress's office to find out which schools they were posted too, some girls ran into classrooms in despair to cry because they were posted to some bad schools all thanks to their grades. Emmy couldn't bare going to see her results so she asked her friend Mpange to go with her, she was nervous and her heart was beating really fast, her head was aching and her face was pale; she did not have the courage to go and find out which school she was posted to. She always wanted to go to Liluni; an Adventist school in the southern province because it produced good results and she had some friends there but she wasn't sure if she had qualified to go there. She held her friends hand tightly, her hands were sweaty and she staggered as she walked toward the headmistress' office. One, two, three steps forward then she stopped and leaned against the wall besides her,

"I can't" she said,

"Don't worry, you have done fine, I know it..."

"I'm too afraid,"

"What are you afraid of?"

"What if I didn't make it anywhere and I'm sent to some really poor school?"

"Emmy, I never did so well remember but I came back here, and I know I will graduate with flying colours."

"You are smart, I'm not."

"I'm not smart, I'm just a hard worker and so are you. Now..." Mpange said as she pulled Emmy off the wall, "Let's go get your results."

They reached the door of the headmistress office where they found a line of girls waiting to collect their results. Emmy and Mpange were third in line, they waited for a few minutes, the anxiety was bothering Emmy; she was anticipating all the negative outcomes...she felt afraid, then there was a loud call 'NEXT' and the girls rushed into the office, the headmistress was very old with a grumpy face that lacked expression but had a constant look of confidence,

"Name?" she asked in a deep horsy voice.

"Emmmm….." Emmy stammered, "Emily sorry, Emmy Lengwe." Then the headmistress filed several sheets of paper with a precise gaze and somewhat looked at the girls through her spectacle, she licked her finger and flipped through again then she paused, turned back a page and pinned it on the table.

"Aha, mwana (child) you did not do so well but you did not do so badly either, so we are keeping you here because we believe we can help you, you will definitely do better in the next exams if we push you." She said as she tried to encourage her, Emmy simple nodded as she received the result form and stuffed it in her bag, she was sad and she turned slowly; Mpange was sceptical and asked,

"Sorry Madam, what is her number," then the headmistress reluctantly read out her exam ID as if to prove a point,

"Ahh, I knew it. That's her twin sister."

"Twin sister?? The headmistress asked as she filliped a few more pages and laughed, "Mmmm" she said with a smile, "This one is going to Lilui Adventist High School."

Emmy couldn't believe it, she froze as the headmistress' voice echoed in her ear, she stood still facing Mpange who then looked at her and ran towards her lifting her as she hugged her, she was overwhelmed with so much joy she could barely breath, Mpange rushed to collect her results and she showed them to Emmy as they skipped out of the headmistress' office,

"Look at your grades, they are amazing…wow, I told you that you would do good. You've been accepted, mmm now you get to school with Sheba," Mpange said referring to her elder brother.

As they walked down the corridors they meet Emily who Emmy then quickly gave her the results form stuffed in her bag she continued walking. Emily looked at her results then she folded her paper again "Eish….how will I explain this" she said to herself, then she walked out of the school premises lighting a cigarette on her way.

It was the beginning of a new year, Mr and Mrs Lengwe had saved so much money so that they could equip their daughter for boarding school, they were not comfortable with sending their daughter to a faraway school with her health condition but they could not deny her of something she so much wanted and earned, they took some precaution like paying a clinic near her school in advance for her health insurance, Emmy was so excited about the school, she had heard so many stories about it from her friends elder brother and she knew all the good students went there; it also had a college where she wanted to do her nursing career. Emily on the other hand did not really care much about which school she went to, her poor grades did not bother her either, she had a theory that her sister was favoured or maybe their results were swapped, the same way she thought they were swapped at birth, she never believed she was the younger sister, even though the difference in minutes of their birth really did not make a difference, she hated how her sister was making such a big fuss about going to boarding school, she hated the idea of boarding school; she felt it to be a prison where parents would send their children out of stress.

"It's a good thing you are staying, I need to keep a close eye on you," Mrs Lengwe said to Emily; she was helping Emmy fold her clothes into a suitcase. Emmy was so busy ironing her uniforms and the clothes she would wear the following day. It was the evening before Emmy left for boarding school.

"I don't get it, you will be trapped in the middle of nowhere, no TVs, no internet, no proper food and you are excited…?" Emily asked her sister with her legs scratching the polished concrete floor as she helped her sister pack groceries into her trunk.

"Emily, when will you ever learn that quality is better than quantity?"

"Quantity of what???"

"Ohhh, you two…this is the last day you will be together and all you can do is debate, ohh. My beautiful twins," their mother said as she cuddled them together, "hmm, you've both grown so much and I'm proud of you, both, Emmy you have proved that nothing will stop you not even your weaknesses and Emily, you are very strong but sometimes your strength is dangerous and I do not trust you so now that your sister is leaving just know that I will deal with you." The words of their mother were loud and clear, same words that left different impressions on each of them, Emily felt threatened and she was afraid she would be discovered, now that all the attention would be on her, she felt a sudden cold chill in her body whilst Emmy felt encouraged and was now even more ready to go into boarding school.

I have always dreamt I have always hoped to be more than me to be free
to be able to reach my destiny, no fear no tear but courage.
To stand on my own feet and not be defined by my
weakness but to be identified by my strengths,
they say I was natures failed experiment.
That my brain worked to slow and that my heart would never last
long enough but now I have improved from where I began.
I might not be gifted nor intelligent, I range somewhere between below
average and challenged but I refuse to accept the reality of these and
I look beyond what is to what could be and there I see me.
Stronger, braver smarter…more beautiful and wiser. I choose to refuse
the life written for me, I WILL PIONEER MY OWN.

The next day came faster than expected. Emmy woke up with anxiety and nausea, she acted like everything was fine because she did not want to scare anyone. She woke up right on time as if she had an alarm clock in her head, to her surprise her sister woke up earlier than her and was busy preparing breakfast for her.

"Oohh, how sweet you're preparing something for me?" Emmy asked.

"Uhhm, I am celebrating your departure." Emily responded.

"Well then, I am equally celebrating my departure from you." Emmy responded as she dashed off to take her bath. Their parents woke up shortly after and began to help Emmy load her bags onto their car. Mr Lengwe took it to a mechanic the previous day to ensure it would not break down, it was constantly breaking down. He had the car for more than ten years constantly fixing it on his own because it was all he could afford; he was saving to buy a new car imported from China but because Emmy had been accepted to an expensive school he used the money to pay for her fees.

"Let's go," Mr Lengwe said as he looked at his daughter. Deep within him was fear at the same time he was so proud of his daughter, he loved her so much and only wanted to see her reach her full potential, he knew letting go would make her happy. Even though he was worried about her medical condition he did want it to prevent her from reaching her dreams. After he had put all the bags on the car he asked everyone to get into the car. Emily walked hesitantly to the car, she did not want to admit it but she felt a part of her life being taken from her, the quiet innocence of her sister made her always feel happy.

He had his hands on the steering, He had never gripped it so tightly, and "So are we good to go?" He asked in his horsy morning voice.

"Wait Bashi Mpundu (father of twins) we need to say a prayer first." Mrs Lengwe said, she then bowed her head and prayed for the journey and her two girls. It was a long journey, they started off early in the morning.

It was a long trip, they went past hills, mountains and villages. There was silence in the car for a while, Emmy and Emily stared out of their windows whilst their parents looked straight ahead. Each one of them had separate thoughts on their mind. Mr Lengwe was deep in thought, he wished there was a way he could turn the car around and force his daughter to attend day school but he was not dictator; he believed in free will, for the first time he wished it was Emily who would go, he wondered who would take care of his daughter.

Fifteen degrees left before the Sun went away, it was not there to stay but its golden rays and warm gaze made the yellow grass glow, in the Savannah did they grow . There was a gentle breeze that carried the scent of dried grass, and here and there you could smell the water of the rivers that split across landscapes.

Mountains and hills cut through the view, with birds returning to their nest, they sang as they flew. The beautiful African sky was lit with red, blue and orange. It was a silent journey a few villages here and there; children playing near their communities and long Savannah grass everywhere.

The land was green and yellow and the sun sank deeper and deeper into the yellow, all that was left in sight was a little road and on that little road was a little car with two little girls, and their parents.

Finally after a long trip they arrived in a community known as Lilui, the first thing they saw was an old, rusted poster written Lilui township, then there was a market and they stopped there for a while because Mrs Lengwe wanted to buy some mushrooms. They continued their journey and after a thirty minute drive, they finally arrived at the school, they were not the only ones, many other new students had arrived and were busy being directed but the teachers on duty. Mr Lengwe quickly stepped out of the car and he was greeted by a teacher.

"Hello Sir, I am Mr Lengwe and I am here to drop off my daughter Emmy" he said as he extended his hand. The teacher shook his hand and responded, "You are welcome Mr Lengwe, please follow me and fill in some paper work, and the prefects will show her the dormitory." Then the teacher looked around and shouted to some pupil who was passing by, "eh, take them to her dorm."

Emily, Mrs Lengwe and Emmy were then escorted to the dormitories by the pupil.

"Hmmm, it's not so bad," Emily said,

"It's perfect!" Emmy exclaimed, they then took a quick tour around the school. Mr Lengwe caught up with them and it was already getting late.

"I spoke to the teachers about your condition" he said, then he kept quiet and in a low voice said, "take care of yourself Mama." Mrs Lengwe hugged her and she was very emotional. "I will miss you" she said. Emily also hugged her sister and said, "don't come back early." Then Mrs Lengwe smacked Emily and in her defence Emily said, "I meant she shouldn't get suspended.

"Your sister would never get suspended," Mrs Lengwe said. After they said their goodbyes, they left the school and Emily was taken to her dormitory by a female teacher.

"Make sure you pack-up and sleep, tomorrow school opens but you can have the day off to pack your things if you are not done by tonight. Come to my office after lunch so that I may show you the clinic." The teacher told her.

Emmy then walked the rest of the way to her dormitory, she felt a sudden chill of cold and loneliness, it was only then that she realised that she had been left alone in a strange place for the first time. She wanted to get her packing done early so that she could go to school the next day, after all she did not have much. When she got back to her cubicle she found another huge suitcase and other bags next to hers, she moved closer to study the suitcase then a girl popped out of nowhere, "Hi!" she exclaimed, "I'm Dorothy Moonga, my dad is pastor Haswell Moonga," she said with a bright expression, Emmy looked surprised. "What? You don't know him, he held that crusade in South Africa and baptised 1000+ people,"

"Ah…, nice to meet you," Emmy simply said to avoid the topic of the Pastor she never heard of, she extended her hand but the girl pulled her and hugged her. Then two girls in a senior looking uniform walked in.

"Hello welcome to Lilui Adventist High School, my name is Chileshe Moyo and I am the dorm prefect I only have one rule, follow the rules," one of the girls said,

"Be sure to attend your orientation tomorrow night at the assembly hall, my name is Martha and I am the surroundings prefect," said the other girl who had a distinct small voice. Then they both walked out and proceeded to the next cubicle.

"The hair…" the prefect whispered to her friend,

"Wait for tomorrow" her friend said

Emmy was no longer feeling so enthusiastic she felt a little afraid but her friend wouldn't stop smiling so she thought to herself that she had no reason to feel afraid.

Meanwhile her parents were taking their long trip back home and it was really getting late.

"Don't worry my cousin leaves in the next town," Mr Lengwe told his wife.

"What's wrong?" Emily asked,

"Nothing dear, I just need to rest. We will spend the night at your uncle's house." Then they travelled for another hour and stopped at a relative of Mr Lengwe's to spend a night. They were welcomed so kindly, Mr Lengwe's sister in-law had prepared for them a nice meal and served them immediately they arrived.

"So, why didn't you bring Emily here as well?" Mr Lengwe's brother James Lengwe asked,

"I am right here..?" Emily answered, then everyone laughed.

"Oh, sorry, Emmy, Emmy." Mr James said correcting his mistake.

"Well we did not want to take her late at night, I had to make somethings clear about her condition." Mr Lengwe responded.

"Ah, well then be sure to give the school my number too, I am nearer to her school, in case of anything, I can get her." He said with a smile.

The room was lit by bulbs that glowed a dim orange, giving of a rusty smell they all sat in the sitting room in brown sofa with a little table on the middle with a plate full of roasted maize(corn) and a tiny CRT TV across the table, Mr Lengwe and his brother stayed there for quite a while telling stories till they decided it was late and they had to rest before his journey back home. Mr Lengwe could not stop thinking about his daughter and how she was.

A fathers love for a little child, my little girl my worry and pride. Now
how will I protect you from this world's merciless tide?
Life is not a fairy-tale and yours is not a story, Good and bad and even wicked are a
deadly reality if I could carry you safety in my arms all the days of your life, I would,
If I would create for you a safer journey and a more secured future how I wish
I could teach you all there is learn and take you around the whole world to see
for yourself the suffering and pain of many, the joy and merry of few.
Those who crush the weak and reach for their blood and those who heal
the sick and give all they have. If I could, I definitely would.
In this world they are wolves and lions, wolves that manipulate and Lions that devour,
how the hours have moved so quickly from the day you were born to today when
you leave me, soon you will leave me completely to build a life of your own.
My only prayer, my only hope is that may the eyes of the Almighty never cease to
look upon you for now you have only one Father, God alone can be with you.

"You are now part of a highly honoured, community who lift the national standards to greater heights, how you do it? Is Hh-up to you, all you have is a brain and a book. Hallow the rules, and h-always keep time." Said a boy elevated on a stage stressing all the 'H's in his sentence, he then sat on a chair on that very stage and someone else stood up.

"Deviance, Dirt, Disobedience….do not dare," She said with her eyes scanning the audience as if searching for something, "Discipline, Cleanliness and Obedience…ahh, we will be friends…" her comments lit up their spirits and some of fresh and young grade ten students seated down below the stage even giggled, "Hey! Who said you could laugh ….you over there," she said pointing at some boy far back in a corner, "Stand up." All the other pupils in the crowd turned to look back at who the prefect was referring to. They were all new pupils in their tenth grade being oriented into a new school, they were anxious…somewhat afraid and one of them being told to stand up made them anxious to what would happen next. She scolded the boy for laughing whilst a prefect was talking, after which she stood up and strolled across the hall as if she was looking for someone, all the juniors were silent, she made a stop somewhere in the middle and asked a girl to stand up.

"Who are you…?" the prefect asked,

"Emm…y" she responded, chocking on her words

"Emmy did you read the school rules before you came here?" She asked and Emmy nodded, then she continued, "Why is your hair treated?"

"It's not…" Emmy responded in despair, then one of the prefects seated next to the prefect standing whispered to her, "it's a weave,"

"So you have a weave?" the prefect asked Emmy. The hall was silent, everyone's attention focused on the egoistic prefect and the unfortunate new girl being interrogated.

"No…" Emmy said with teary eyes ready to pour. Then another female prefect in frustration jumped off the stage headed like a marching bull towards Emmy to further inspect her hair, when she got there she was ashamed to see that she was wrong and that was Emmy's natural hair, it was browner than normal especially under a bright light which made it somewhat glow, she then returned to the stage to redeem herself,

"Weaves are unacceptable, permed hair is unacceptable…dye.." she said staring in Emmy's direction as the word dye came off her lips, She continued to complain about disobedience until the head boy stood up interrupting her and said,

"All in all be good children of God, you are dismissed." And then all the new students quickly evacuated the hallway.

Emmy ran to her blankets and began to cry, her roommate Dorothy climbed up to her patting her lightly and said,

"Don't cry…"

"I'm not crying!" Emmy yelled.

"it's ok, they are just jealous of your hair, besides you were saved by the head boy….he's sooo cuuutee" Dorothy said then Emmy popped out of her blankets and said

"I know right," then they both began to laugh.

Somehow Emmy got through her confrontation, mostly because of Dorothy who supported her she grew fond of Dorothy who reminded her of her dear sister back home. Time flew by and soon the young students adapted to their new environment. The subjects were harder but well taught by the teachers of the school so much time was allocated to studying their books and also devotions.

Because of her health condition Emmy wasn't allowed to do so much work but she tried her best to hide it and performed light duties though prefects did not like her because they could never punish her, she tried her best to stay out of the wrong but because some female prefects had blacklisted her they always looked for a fault in her and tore her apart with their words.

"I don't get it, I thought this was this the best school," Emmy said to her friend who was in the laundry room with her,

"Oh no don't get me wrong Emmy, it's pretty good, that's why they send all the wrong people here…to set them straight."

Then Dorothy came panting in the room, "Emmy, you are wanted outside," she said with a slight smile. Emmy then went outside and to her surprise,

"Hi, Emmy right."

"Yes…" she responded,

"Ok, so I've been hearing a lot about you lately, from my prefects especially…being late, not working or being rude, disobedience." Said the head boy, Emmy tried to pay attention but she could not stop avoiding eye contact with him, his deep dark eyes stared seriously at her and there was something about his lips that made it look like wishes had come true,

"Hello, is there anything you want to say?" he asked her, then she shook her head really quickly as she returned to reality. "So tell me, why do you always run away from the prefects even when they catch you?" He asked.

"I avoid the interrogations and they always look for something wrong, as if they get paid to do so." She responded.

He then giggled a little, "and I hear you never finish work when they punish you."

"I always finish, I Just finish late." She responded.

"Do you know why I am here, when I call you it's either two things a last warning or you are leaving this school, I followed you which means that you little child are walking on ice, ice that can easily break if you waste my time…I do not punish people because that's what my prefects do, what I do is two things, I could either make you the most disciplined student from today onwards or I could send you back home by tomorrow…" he said to her with a very tormenting tone, Emmy was scared, she began to breathe heavily her heart was racing too fast.

"I have, I have a rare case of diabetes, I've had it since I was young. I go to the clinic every evening to ensure that my body is under normal conditions that's why I'm always late for evening Prep, and I work slowly because too much stress might lead to a Pneumomediastinum, I ran away from all the prefects because they scare me and always stress me out." She responded with gaps in her sentences.

"Why don't you tell them that you are sick." He asked Emmy who was right now already crying,

"All my life I am known as the sick child, for once I just want to be like everyone else." She said wiping her nose, the head boy stood there just looking at her for a minute, then without a word he simple turned and left. Emmy did not feel threatened by him, at first she was afraid but then she just felt helpless, she wished she had remained with her family at home and that she just complicated her own life now, everybody thought she was rebellious except for those few who really knew her and the head boy was one of them. She did not want to be seen as a sick girl at her new school so she tried her best to conceal her illness but it was not easy.

The little family trip made Emily think a lot, she was afraid of facing any sanctions so she tried to be on her best behaviour; went to school every day, tried her best to stay in class the whole time, even rushed back home early to avoid her gang members, the least thing she wanted her parents discovering her bad habits, she thought they might even send her to an isolated girls school somewhere far, unlike her sister she preferred civilization but her mother was on her trail she knew something was up with her.

It's funny how the days walk by, when you realise it you will see them fly. Time is an element like the wind, it seems so abstract how you can't catch it in your palm or keep it still in a glass bottle no matter how much you want to. Days became years before anyone knows it, sometimes it's too fast other times it's too slow where ever it goes nobody knows the only sad thing is that you can never catch it once it's gone.

He took heavy steps but they were not as heavy as his breathing, his face had changed, his usual soft Ivy face was hard and his forehead had a giant wrinkle, his pupils dilated and his eyebrows curved in. His beautiful moulded body was in motion down the passage he marched taking sharp turns till he arrived at a door with a sign post 'prefects lounge' and he banged the door open taking the attention of all the white shirted pupils with green sashes and pectoral badges. They were terrified, they recognized that look, being the diplomat he was he tried not to yell but even his low tone was as fierce as the growl of a lion.

"Martha," he said,

"Yes Head boy" she responded knowing the usage of her first name signalled a bad temper.

"Why did I miss my biology lab experiment today?" he asked

"I don't…know" she responded looking at her comrades in shock.

"wrong answer, I was up to my usual patrol today when I found a girl lying on the balcony of your dormitory because someone couldn't handle the fact that she is better looking than you can ever be." He answered,

"Head boy that's not why I punished her," she responded,

"Oh but it's just as sarcastic as the real reason you punished her, maybe it's even more realistic." He said, Martha was silent she knew not to answer back because she had punished Emmy for wearing her jersey backward accidentally.

"Power is not meant to be played with for all Authority comes from God and in the end we all answer to him, so I missed Biology because I carried a diabetic girl to the clinic early in the morning and only got back now because she is only a little stable."

"I didn't know,"

"You should know," then the head boy approached her and pulled off her badge throwing it to her friend who sat close to her.

"Chipala I'm sorry, please don't do this, I'll apologize." Martha said with tears in her eyes,

"Oh yes you will apologize, but forget about being a prefect." Chipala, the Head Boy told her, then he took one step back, looked at all the prefects in the room with his blood lit eyes, and walked out of the door into the hallway. Martha remained there crying, she was so ashamed that she ran out of the room.

The next day in the morning Emmy was carrying her bucket into the showers where she drew water from a tap, there was no one in the showers that time because all the girls went for breakfast after which they would go for class. Emmy was had been sick the previous day so she woke up later than everyone, she was still feeling a slight headache but ignored it, then she heard footsteps, she wandered who it was, everyone had evacuated the dormitory. A girl walked in with a towel, Emmy tried her best not to stare directly at her because she feared it might be a prefect but she could feel the girl was looking at her, Emmy slightly turned her head to catch a glimpse of the girl standing by the other tap….it was Martha, she felt her insides turn.

"Morning Prefect Martha," she said.

Martha simply rolled her huge eyes at her and walked out of the showers leaving her bucket drawing water. Emmy did not hesitate to take her shower, she took it as fast as she could and dressed up even quicker, she did not even bother to go and eat because she did not want to meet any prefects who would question her about being late for breakfast, so she decided just to go straight to her class, on her way there she meet Chipala who was doing one of his patrols. As the head boy he would patrol the school three times a day to make sure everything was in order. During his patrols no one, not even prefects would be moving around; all the prefects would be stationed at their posts and the pupils either quiet in class, quiet in their dorms or quiet at the dining hall. The school seemed empty at that moment, if scary. What scared the ordinary students most was bumping into him when he was patrolling, anyone who ever did was in big trouble, that's why Emmy stumbled when she saw him, she tried to hide from him then she heard,

"Emmy…" he said in a calm voice which made her stand still, Emmy turned and only imagined what she had gotten herself into, she tried to invent reasons for why she was loitering at the sports pitch when she was supposed to be in the cafeteria, what separated the class area from the dormitory area was the sports pitch which was being renovated by a generous donation from a basketball championship the school had won, she thought of what to say but she couldn't say it.

"How are you feeling?" he asked, then Emmy's pupils dilated and constricted at the same time,

"The nurse gave me an injection and said I should go for another one today," she responded hesitantly,

"Ok, but how are you?" He asked again, this time drawing closer to her,

"I think I'm fine," she said

"You won't be getting any trouble from my prefects any longer but in case of anything... they should pray you don't find me first," he said as he walked on passed her but she stayed still not quiet understanding what he said or meant, she shook her head and then rushed to her classroom.

Later that day, a class was having a History lesson with half of the class either absent minded or asleep, the teacher sat on a teacher table in front reading from a book the history of the Mthethwa people. She seemed to be teaching but the class was far too tired to pay attention, they were in their final year and already had so much to read.

"Hey," some girl in a blue shirted uniform whispered to a girl leaning against a wall with far too much make-up.

"Martha..." she continue to whisper until Martha faced her direction,

"Is it true?" the girl asked Martha,

"Yea," Martha responded frustrated,

"Why?" the girl continued to question her,

"Some girl reported me for abusing her...imagine some grade ten..." Martha said,

"Which girl," the girl asked,

"Eh, Sampa...leave me alone," Martha told her frustrated.

"Is it that girl with the weave, hmmm? Her and the head boy, I even saw them together this morning," Sampa told her, making Martha focus her full attention on her,

"You saw them together?" Martha asked,

"Yes!" Sampa told her,

"Huh Martha, bad bad girl, because you like him," Sampa said,

"Iwe, I don't like that boy...he's too serious." Martha defended herself. Martha thought to herself, she conceived devious ideas in her head, she couldn't handle that she had been demoted not for such a ridiculous reason she thought.


Emmy's secret was finally out, everyone knew about her condition, everyone finally understood her; why her eye colour was slightly milder and changed from time to time, why she could never get her work done in time, why she would be weaker than most...they could see her better and no one bothered her anymore but she did not like being looked at as someone who is experiencing a life threating medical condition; she was fine provided she never missed any treatment and followed all her lifestyle requirements. People talked about her and she tried her best to avoid the spotlight being a shy girl, she often spent her time in the Library, there she was invited to be a librarian and do her duties from there, but that was a string that Chipala had secretly pulled for her because he knew being duty less would make the prefects dislike her more.

'I live in a world where people choose to look with their eyes,
If only they would see with their heart and judge with
their souls, really inside we are all the same;
sick or healthy, short or tall white or black we all look the same on the inside,
no one wrote an application letter to be what they are but God gave them what he saw was fit,
but Lord is this what fits me, I smell like insulin and look as pale as the moon my
body is weak and my eyes are losing their strength my stature tiny…oh well,
today I will hide in the world of history and Anatomy, I will clear these
tables and dust these books for tomorrow I take on the world!'

Suddenly there was clapping from a figure behind,

"Wow, beautiful poem, except there was something wrong…you don't smell like insulin, you smell like…..well, books."

Emmy then quickly climbed down the ladder she was using to stack some books on a shelf,

"Chipala! I mean…Head boy. What are you doing here?" she asked him shyly,

"Head Boy…is my head that big?" he asked her with a smile, she felt uncomfortable about him being so informal.

"Uuhm, I was studying but you see I was disturbed by someone reciting a poem,"

"Hmm, I was not reciting, that was original,"

"Ohh, really?" He asked her

"Yes really," she responded

"Ok, so you are a poet?" he asked

"No…not really, I think its part of how this story goes…" she said unconfidently, somewhat confused, "anyway…this is my world here in the library, so I'm free to do whatever"

"Your world, and how exactly did it become your world?" he asked her,

"Well, I visit it often and the senior Librarian noticed my skills and made me one of the librarian here plus my grades did all the talking," she said so confidently dusting her shoulders.

Chipala laughed, "Is that so? Fine, well this is my school and the library is in my school. So, tell me Librarian, what kind of books do you read?"

"Well, I read everything but I particularly enjoy Anatomy," she told him as he slowly pulled one of the chairs from the desk and sat on it,

"And why's that?" he asked curiously,

"Well, my dad once told me sometimes a problem is the answer to another problem…maybe I'm in my condition to help others in my condition, "she said looking at the floor then he began to giggle and she stopped talking,

"It's not funny," she said looking annoyed,

"No, no its not, it's just that, see, when my young brother was a baby he had an infection that affected his body, it had some treatment that was too expensive; here in Zambia, my parents by then weren't so privileged as they are now, they struggled raising money to help him, but by the time they had even half the amount… half of his body became paralysed, so since then, all I've wanted is to become a medical doctor, he is my vision my mission my aim and my drive, I never let anything distract me, maybe there's a way to make him walk again…" Chipala lost his voice and feared that his laughter might turn into tears if he continued talking. Emmy knew he was in pain so she tried to divert him, "well, I would love to study medicine too but I can't if I don't solve this chemical equation," she then sat on the chair next to him and showed him a random question in the textbook she was previously reading, he looked at her as she attempted to show him questions he was sure she was not learning so he simply smiled and played along.

"No, that's not how it happened, anyway, I'm getting sleepy, let me check the time so that, MY WEH!!! Its 03:00." Emmy said so surprised,

"So?" Chipala asked her,

"Haaa, how did, when did, I'm so late, wonder if…"

"Relax, I sleep at 4 everyday studying,"

"And what time do you wake up?" she asked him,

"07:00, for my patrols….sometime 08:00"

"Haa, you're a senior…oh no, it's so late, I better go," she said,

"Ok, let me escort you"

"NO!! I'll just go," she said,

"Ok, good luck walking through that dark pitch, you know it being renovated so if you fall into a ditch don't scream for help because then, that'll definitely wake everyone up and you'll be in trouble."

"Librarians are allowed to spend nights studying in the library," she boasted as she grabbed her books and stuffed them in her bag half on her way out of the Library,"

"True, except…this is not night, its early morning and a ditch wouldn't be a library." Chipala said standing up and stretching.

A girl from one of the girls dormitory was up sending messages to her boyfriend when she heard footsteps outside, she quickly stuffed her phone in between a loaf of bread fearing it might be prefects having a phone search, she then looked outside her window to analyse the situation then suddenly her mouth fell wide open and she pulled out her phone from the loaf and sent a text to a her friend Cynthia who forwarded it to Mundia who forwarded it to Given who forwarded it to Sampa who forwarded it to Martha who upon reading it stood up and went to a small studying cubicle where her successor sat studying.

"What Martha," she asked irritated by the disturbance

"Where is Emmy?" Martha said

"What's this all about Martha,"

"Patricia, you as the dorm and surroundings prefect needs to know where everyone is," Martha told her folding her hands

"Ha! If you were so good why were you sacked," Patricia told her, Martha then pulled her and dragged her to the end of the dormitory where the grade tens had their cubicles, particularly Emmy's banker and Martha began to wake Dorothy, Emmy's bunk mate, up. She then woke up very surprised and when they asked her where Emmy was she answered that she was probably studying at the library; Patricia was so irritated and walked back to her cubicle, she was wearing her glasses and a sleeping gown, on her way there she met Emmy at the door of the dormitory,

"Where are you from?" she asked her,

"The library." Emmy responded

"Who were you with?" she was asked,

"…I was alone but, the Head Boy was also studying there," she said

"Next time, don't come back after 01," Patricia told her as she headed back to her cubicle and Emmy rushed to her bed, Martha felt furious as she watched what happened, she felt that a great injustice was done, what was so special about Emmy that nobody wanted to punish her for all she had done. Martha went back to Patricia's cubicle more angry than before. She told Patricia that she needed to discipline Emmy because Emmy was so stubborn and grew big-headed when she was pardoned, Patricia tried to reason with her that she was misdirecting her anger for being dropped and this was no longer her area of interest.

"Ok, it's not! But that girl if you are not careful will also get you in trouble, it's just a matter of time, she needs to be stopped." Martha said with his feet sinking into the concrete.

"I'd rather leave her alone Martha," Patricia said,

"Wait till all her friends start acting like her, just because she is seeing the head boy should she undermine a senior prefect like you?" Martha said,

"Ok, so what should I do?" Patrice asked Martha in frustration, and then Martha just grinned.

Emily was slaving over the stove trying to cook dinner, ever since Emmy had left she had to do all the work at home and it was stressful but at least she was busy and she stayed away from trouble, she was cooking a local meal that required a lot of power and she was trying so hard to stir the mixture, her pants were even falling off but they were pulled back up so roughly by her mother who just entered the kitchen returning from work,

"Mum!" She yelled pulling out headsets from her ears,

"Why are you doing it like that?" her mother asked

"Aahh, it's so hard!" Emily responded,

"You make it hard, Emmy always made it soft, and if your pants are falling off wear a skirt," her mother told her,

"Uhh mum, its swag," Emmy said whispering to herself.

"Eeeh, what's that!" her mother said as she grabbed the cooking stick Emmy was using to cook the nsima (the traditional meal) and started to beat her with it.

Emily went to school the next day with her face swollen, "Hey, Emily ehhhh! What happened?" one of her classmates asked her,

"Mum went all gangster on me," she told him,

"Ah, I know what will make you feel better," he said as he pulled something from his pocket.

"No ways, you won't me to look worse than this." She told him pointing at her face.

Her fear of being found out was keeping her from doing drugs but because she was so used to them she was starting to have withdrawal symptoms. She could not hold it much longer.

The silence was golden except for a two students who were laughing, it was late in the library and Emmy was studying there and so was Chipala but they found themselves telling jokes from nowhere. She somehow found refuge in the old school library and it was somehow always better when Chipala was there, he rarely studied from there but when he did they would always laugh about what happened during the week, and he had a special way of turning an intimidating situations into jokes and Emmy found them so hilarious, she couldn't stop laughing. She was paying so much attention to him as he talked looking so anxiously at him as she waited for each word to come out of his mouth, each funnier than the prior. For some reason the head boy was no longer an intimidating figure that she tried to avoid, he was now a friend and her favourite prefect. Then whilst he was talking she remembered her friends' advice; how they warned her to keep her distance from the head boy, because the seniors were jealous and most of the prefects thought she was dating him so she sat upright and moved her chair back, "I need to go," she simply told him standing up abruptly,

Suddenly he was compelled to hold her arm, he seemed intense and she was startled, then he let go of her hand and she had to leave the library so she quickly packed her books throwing them in her bag and she checked her watch repeatedly rushing and feeling very strange, Chipala watched her every move because he could not understand her, Emmy quickly waved at him and when she opened the main library door she found a group of prefects and the boarding master just outside whispering to each other… Emmy froze, Chipala who was seated on the table felt a shift in her stature, she was still and somewhat pale and in the blink of an eye he rushed towards her worried to his surprise he met five of his prefects standing the other side of the door with the boarding master, by the look of things he knew exactly what was happening.

In the miniscule of a second, his perspective changed and he realised that what he thought he had, what he thought he knew was in a conflict to keep what he had so long had fought for.

He knew he had enemies in his flock, those who at his achievements had remorse,
those who would not look back when given the knife to stab his back,
those who longed for what power and influence he had and those who wanted to be
with him but would never have him, he felt angry after everything he did to keep
them on their podium they returned to him this...pandemonium, all the power and
influence that lay in his hand, was now a feeble stick that he held in his mouth.

Chipala was doing so well, he knew something like this would happen eventually; he was the Head prefect, his grades were great, he was even short-listed for a University scholarship and on top of all that, many teachers offered to help him look for a job after he graduated. His friends were jealous of him especially some of the prefects but it still hurt him to see what those he trusted cooked up for him.

"Chipala, how long has this been going on?" the Boarding Master asked him.

"3 years Sir, that's how long I've been studying late at the Library and the librarians, Sir, they can stay here till midnight." Chipala said as he looked directly in the direction of the prefects who were with the Boarding Master.

"Its 02:00" the Boarding master said looking at his watch. "The Deputy's office tomorrow, 08:00," he continued.

Chipala was left in the library as the two female prefects walked Emmy to her dorm and the rest went with the boarding master. He looked down at his watch...it was two hours and thirty minutes behind...how did that happen? He also remembered that for some reason, Emmy's watch was not working today.

Hours later,

There was silence in the dormitory, it was still empty until girls started walking in, each making a turn at her cubicle and setting or laying down on her bed, Dorothy was in in such a rush, all the girls looked at her when she ran past them...she went to her cubicle and there she found Emmy seated on her little suitcase.

"What happened?" she asked Emmy, Emmy sat there still and only spoke with her tears, Dorothy was angry and she yelled whilst trying to control herself, "Emmy! Tell me what they said," but Emmy cried even more and Dorothy fell on her knees holding Emmy's hands trying to console her and giving her hope but deep within Emmy's eyes, there was no hope.

"They accused me of dating Chipala, they…they had photos and witness it was so confusing, they were not after me though…Dorothy they were after him and his badge and," Emmy put her hand on her mouth and shivered when she tried to talk,

"Except for that witch! She hated you from the first day, she just wants her revenge!" Dorothy said with tears in her eyes.

"No, but…the others they connived to try and get rid of him, she almost got me expelled… she called me rude and a bad influence and a who…" Emmy said choking on her words "he stepped down, when, they were about to expel me he took all the blame and then threw his captain sash on the floor and he left the room. He did it to keep me at this school, he…he threw it all away, but I'm not coming back Dorothy, I hate this school, I can't…I can…haaa, eeh." As she was speaking, Martha walked into the cubicle and looked at Emmy.

"I warned you, look at what you have done now. I'm sorry," she said with a sad face and then as she left she put on a grin.

"How did I get here?" Emmy asked herself.

> When things go wrong the clock ticks so fast you wonder how you got from
> A to B, three months ago I was leaving home with dreams and expectations,
> now I'm back I don't even know how I got here. My heart has never beat so
> fast but this is not the time to faint…because I might not wake up.

'This chair has never felt so hard, and Emily just picked the worst time to be discovered…I thought she had stopped, look at us, no different from each other. We are both seated on this couch waiting to be judged.'

Mrs Lengwe walked in the house so furiously and slapped Emmy and Emily both at once, she was so angry. "Wait here," she told them as she headed to the kitchen to get a cooking stick which she would use to smack them. She could not stop herself from yelling as she smacked them.

"I should have had boys instead. Do you know the sacrifices me and your father have made to keep you alive…this one is doing drugs the other one!" she said. Mr Lengwe just stood by the door but he when he saw his wife sweating and shivering he rushed and tried to calm her down.

"Bana Mpundu (mother of twins)…" he told her,

"Don't call me by their names!" She yelled.

"you need to calm down….no….for your sake just calm down" he said as he tried to hold her but she forced herself out of his hands and stood in front of her daughters…she looked at them in horror and she said, "How did you get here?" with tears in her eyes and then suddenly she started coughing vigorously and blood come out o her mouth as she did, she grew short of breath and she fell to the ground and passed out. She was rushed to the hospital but she did not get there soon enough. In two weeks, they buried her.

> Death is like a wormhole that will take anything and anyone at any time
> regardless of who they are what they do or how much money they have.
> Never satisfied is the grave, so jealous that it takes what you love sometimes it
> won't even let you say good bye, won't even care however you cry, won't let one
> repent, when it takes it does not relent. Oh, the way it comes when you least
> expect it, if you could pay to buy time but it has no price, all it wants is life.
> She had more to say more reason to stay, so much she had worked for
> that she would have, could have and should have enjoyed.
> What a painful life to live in suffering and poverty everyday looking forward to
> better day but death took all that away, only to die in suffering and poverty.

They threw roses on her wooden bed where she lay, roses she craved when she could still smile when she smelt their spring scent but now all you could see on her face was horror and a face that lost its definition.

"Dear Lord,

I don't understand why you took her away? Was it to punish me for everything I've done. But why? Did you take her when you knew everyone else would suffer...why not just punish me instead, Dad and Emmy did not deserve this, maybe Emmy a little but she already paid her price when she got suspended. Why did you make her suffer like this, she was a good woman she did not deserve to be suffering, I had no idea she had High Blood pressure, and you revealed it to us in such a way??? Look I have no one else to turn to Ok, but...I need someone to talk to! And I hear you can resurrect people so please bring her back....please, please....I promise, I'll stop everything I do, I'll quit the drugs, for good this time and I'll, I'll start praying, I'll start going to church.

Can you hear me...I said I'll stop it all...hey! Answer me! Are you even real? Why don't you step down and face me right now! If they say you love this world then why do you allow such things to happen why do you take people away like this?

Ohh, so you choose to be silent, fine! Be silent, but you must know that I would do anything to have my mother back....anything! I'm for real, look I'm here kneeling in your church right now, I had to jump through a window just to get in but I'm here alright and I'm for real... are you?"

"Emily," said a calm voice from the back.

"There is a time for everything, but you know your mother loved you despite everything." Her father said as he walked towards her; he had been looking for her everywhere and this was the least place he expected to find his mourning daughter, it had been a week since his wife had died and he too had been greatly disturbed, she was the closest family he had and the joy of his youth, losing her was a blow, he was angry with his daughters for their misconduct but he knew they needed comfort and love more than ever.

"You are just saying that," Emily said still kneeling in front of a pulpit.

"Life doesn't end with death," Mr Lengwe said as he held his daughters together tears flooding the church.

"Yes, that's true," said a very old man was silently watching what was happening and he finally decided to intervene

"Death is not the end, it's a little sleep, a little slumber but one day when we all wake up
at the sound of the archangel…we will understand it. For now we cannot comprehend
why everything happens but trust the words of the Lord my dear ." He continued.

Then told the family to kneel down and he said a short word of prayer for them then he shared a few verses with them which helped but both girls said they wanted to see their mother again, the pastor told them there was a way they could, if they gave their lives to Jesus Christ and got baptised they were assured to have a better end in heaven. That's how they would get there.

# Chapter 5

## *Where the rivers meet*

The narrow corridors crossed each other like little streams each leading to separate wards. It was all white and had a peculiar smell that was not bad but not good either. The air had a peculiar medicine smell that was fighting the peachy air freshener. Close to the doors were benches which leaned on the hallway walls, a number of people sat there waiting to be attended to, they all shared one thing in common; a face of despair and sickly looking bodies, only the nurses looked somewhat healthy but all in all they were all tired except for a woman who sat in the reception; with her gloved hands that were holding a newspaper. Her legs were crossed, she wore beautiful cream-white heels with a red base, her body streamlined with a beautiful midnight blue dress and besides her was a hand bag; after flipping a number of pages she stood up hastily and approached the receptionist.

"Hello Mrs, I've been waiting for a long time now." She said to the receptionist,

"Wait Madam, the Director is very busy." The receptionist responded not even looking at her,

The lady then walked back to the bench and shortly after she was called into the Directors office. She quickly stood up pulling her bag and rushed into his office before she could miss the opportunity. Her heart was beating, she was anxious and afraid at the same time so she sucked her lips and held her breath as she was closing the door and when she turned facing him, she wore a confident smile.

"Hello," she said shaking his hand the director took a quick look at her and stared down on some papers, they had a short conversation where he interviewed her and tried to get some information about her,

"Well," he said, "your papers are very impressive Miss but I don't think you are what we are looking for," he told her plainly.

"I'm sorry," she was very surprised, "what more are you looking for?"

Jane Jamila Nakasamu

"We have hired a number of people who have proved too irresponsible and this is a state of the art hospital, there are only three like this so, we are quiet strict with our selection." He told her,

She was still in shock and shook her head saying, "I am more than qualified than most of the people here, I worked with the Army for five years and I have dealt with more delicate issues than this hospital can fathom so tell me, what more do you want?" She asked him,

"We want assurance and integrity, Miss now, please leave, I have things to do." He told her

"Assurance? Integrity? Huh, I think I know what this is all about, you just want to hire those men I saw earlier who came here even later than I did, you know I was the only volunteer who went to work as a Doctor with the Peace keepers all the other men either Quit or got killed" she said narrowing her eyes towards him and she continued, " I lost my mother about 15 years ago from what could have been prevented by the Doctors of this country and my dad had to work so hard for me to study Medicine in fact my sister sacrificed Law school in order for me to complete my studies and I have always done more than people anticipate of me, what can you tell me about Assurance and Integrity, you know what, I'll just speak to the Senior Director," she said as she stood up and stormed out of his office. She marched down the hallway towards the Senior Directors office and he ran after her trying to stop her. When she reached his office she opened the door and immediately placed her demands, she was furious, this was the fifth hospital to turn down her application after she finished her contract with the army mostly some debt issues led to the lack of employment in the country but she felt that the country owed her for her brave service. The senior Director was silent, he was amazed all he could say was "Dr Bwalya, please excuse us." telling the Director and the Director left the office immediately. After she had finished complaining he did not say anything, she wondered what was wrong with him,

"You have the job," he said,

She was surprised a bit ashamed so she tried not to stay in his office for too long but as she made her way out he asked her "What's your name?"

"Dr Emmy Lengwe." She said humbly.

She walked out of his office very silent, she felt a bit different than before she stormed into his office, she began to replay the whole scene in her mind, she pictured herself walking into his office, her breathing was heavy and her bag was swinging, behind her was the other Director and he was trying to stop her but she was a woman on a mission that no one could stop. She remembered looking at him and beginning to tell him that it was embarrassing that his Hospital had a policy that preferred hiring men to women then she talked about her at the Army despite her own Medical condition, then she remembered how he sat upright when he heard that and she also remembered that he had a strange look on his face. His office was filled with so many books and certificates that she only noticed now when she began to recall. She then remembered

36

continuously pointing at the other Director who was standing behind her, the Senior Director then asked the other Director to leave and she talked a little calmer but still seriously saying that she had all it took to work at the Hospital. She still felt there was something strange the conversation, 'is it because I was the only one talking? ' She asked herself, she blamed herself for complaining too much and making it awkward. Before she knew it she was parked in front of an Apartment block, she quickly climbed up the stairs, dusting her coat on her way up, it accumulated dust from her car which she hadn't drove in a long time. She reached in front of a door with the number 284 on it, she searched her bag for her phone and made a phone call. It was ring for a while then the door was opened abruptly, it was opened by a woman of her age, very beautiful but clearly stress made her look older than her age,

"Why didn't you pick up?" Emmy asked

"Didn't want to waste your talk time, come in." she said

Emmy walked in slowly continuously looking around at the room that was very untidy, her host cleared a few blankets off a chair and placed them on a table right next to a dirty mug that 5-day-old coffee stains, Emmy had a worried look on her face as she looked around.

"What?" her host asked her,

"Nothing, it's just…how are you Emily?" Emmy asked.

"Same way you left me, didn't even let me know you were back, Lucy told me she saw you running around hospital hallways…" Emily said as she began to eat what was left of her nsima (the traditional meal), she did look unhappy and Emmy saw that.

"Do you want some?" Emily asked her sister,

"No thank you, sorry I didn't come earlier I just wanted to find a job first…didn't want to burden you by asking to live with you,"

"Good thing you know that," Emily said half smiling whilst bended still eating her food,

"How is work?" Emmy asked Emily,

"Uh, I almost got laid off, they had some tax issued and had to pay some debt but I negotiated my stay."

"Huh this debt thing is killing us, you're always so fierce, hmm"

"So did you get yourself a job?"

"Well, actually, I did but,"

"But?" Emily asked looking at her sister with her huge tired eyes,

"I don't know something strange happened today, I got rejected after my interview but I complained to the senior Director and I got the job."

"Wait, how is that a bad thing?" Emily asked,

"Well it was weird," Emmy told her,

"Hmmm, what's weird is how little they pay accountants these days, I mean we are the ones making all the money…take the job, good for you Doctor." Emily said.

"Yea, I guess I will." Emmy responded.

"What did you say was the hospital again?"

"Mwewo Hospital." Emmy responded, they stayed up for a while talking until they both decided they had to sleep, Emmy spent the night at her sister's house, she had nowhere else to go. The next morning before they went to work, they stopped by the graveyard, Emmy wanted to go there then she would drop Emily off at work, Emily did not want to visit the graveyard but she did not have a car so she had no choice.

"I don't like coming here," Emily said, "It's the worst part of my life."

Emmy looked at her sister she did not have any words, she then looked at the graves below, her mothers and her fathers. Their father's death was tragic he had an electrical accident and the intensity of it was so bad that is was in the newspapers six years ago; it was a big court case with the electrical company. The company offered to pay for the education of both daughters of Mr Lengwe in compensation but it did not make life any easier. The past fifteen years for Emmy and Emily were hard, they only had each other and some distant relatives who were not so generous, it was only by grace that they made it thus far, Emily fell into a deep drug addiction a couple of times but she got over it after their father passed, Emmy blamed herself for everything that happened, her sister was kind enough to sacrifice law school in order for her sister to study Medicine, Emily studied accounting at a college instead. Emmy looked at her sister in awe, she was brave that why when she was offered a job to work as a Doctor abroad with the army she also tried to be brave like her lovely sister.

They stood across the graves, Emmy replacing the old flowers with new ones, it was evident that Emily never visited the graveyard but her sister did not condemn her, she understood that Emily did not want to be reminded of what happened but she could never forget.

There was a deep soil smell, accompanied with the smell grass and manure from some of the graves that were richly maintained, the twins looked with heavy hearts, Emmy sat on her mother's grave like a child and she whispered some words to herself, she might have been praying or talking to the concrete. Emily was clearly in deep thought, her face showed a deep remorse. The sky was cloudy and a cold wind blew across the graveyard leaving a chill that further hardened their frozen hearts.

"Ok, let's go." Emily said as she stood up and dusted herself, her sister patted her shoulder and they walked looking only forward.

# Chapter 6

## Uncovering history

After they visited the graveyard, Emmy dropped her sister off at her workplace and proceeded to the hospital. A huge smile lit up her face that Thursday morning as she approached the gate written

'Mwewo Hospital, because we care, Dr Chimboni'

The words bounced on her lips as she read them. It was to be her first day of work and she was quite early. She parked her car and was welcomed by the very Secretary who was rude to her the previous day, the secretary gave her a tour of the hospital and told her that she was expected to attend a meeting every Monday morning. She gazed at the infrastructure as she walked towards the Meeting room, it was a beautiful hospital, one of the best in the country and it was built not long ago. She arrived in the meeting room and sat waiting for it commence. The Senior Doctors arrived and they addressed the others, there was a special respect given to Dr Chimboni, the founder and Senior Director, he gave the closing remarks and even introduced Emmy. She found it strange when he spoke he introduced her like he knew her and he had a special way of articulating that seemed familiar to Emmy and she kept running through her mind as if she knew something then suddenly it hit her, like a bomb, memories flashed back to her and she was as still as a statue. She had known him all this while but did not recognize him. Her feelings were mixed, she did know what to feel. Sudden pain, misdirected anger all her nerves were tingling, she felt a little dizzy but she had trained herself to control her stress even though she needed to vent it, she walked straight towards Dr Chimboni stopping him and yelling, "It's you?" she attracted the attention of all the doctors in the corridor and he signalled that she should follow him to his office, when they got there he could barely sit down when she began talking.

"How could I not see it, what…why didn't you say something, why did you hire me?" she told him

"What was I to do when you were threatening to sue me?" he responded,

"Sue you, no…but at least I had I right to know,"

"I really didn't think you cared, you're the one who just stopped talking to me all those years ago." He said then Emmy left his office and run to the hospital garden where she was so overwhelmed with emotions that she began to cry. She did not know what to do, she was not sure if she would continue working there, how could she, when Chipala brought back all the pain and anger she buried in her past. She looked up to the sky and said a short prayer, "Father, guide me," before she could finish she heard screams nearby and rushed to see what had happened, a woman came running to the hospital with a child who she was saying was dead, Emmy quickly got the child and immediately took her into the hospital for treatment, there she discovered that the child was poisoned and she was able to treat the child…a few hours later the child woke up and what was five hours happened so quickly that it felt like seconds. Emmy was able to save the child and the child's mother was overjoyed,

"Thank you, you're an angel," she told Emmy,

"No. I'm a doctor, it's my job," Emmy said,

"But I don't have money to pay, I live in the nearby ghetto and I'm sure this was no accident," the woman said,

"It's covered," Emmy said,

"Why? How?"

"Because we care, just fill in a form at the reception and put my name at the bottom, here is my card."

That went different than she had expected, there were so many signs telling her to stay, but even more telling her she was still in love with Chipala Chimboni.

Effortlessly I cared,
Why nobody else dared to be the better than what they could be…these people they looked at me, these doctors they mocked me and the nurses laughed at me. Because I dared to care, for a woman with a dying child, a dirty woman and a smelly child, who they asked to go to a general hospital because she could not afford to pay the bill to save the life of her child,
Tell me, what is the cost of life, is it not free, is it costly to care, make a loss when you dare to care and be the better you, you can definitely be. I have watched Generals and Commanders die before my eyes from gunshot wounds, they had all the money but it could not restore their lives.
Life is too short to be greedy.
We might be different on the outside, have different perspectives about life, see the world from different world views, some might own half of the world and others

nothing to call their own. Some might live in houses the size of football stadiums
and others just sleep in a little box during the cold nights but cut them all in half;
rip them all apart and you will discover that we are all the same on the inside.
Just the same.

Everybody stared as a client walked into the office, he was not like all the other clients; they all had the money but he smelt like it, and had the face to go with it. His walk was confident and he bowed when he met someone, his suit was so elegant even the secretary didn't ask him to sign in when he walked passed her his shoes looked like they did walk on the ground, he had a princely stature and the people at the office wondered where he came from, some imagined some nice country abroad, all the ladies stared except for Emily who got angry when she saw him, "What are you doing here?" she asked him aggressively, he simply smiled and said, "relax, I'm a client." as he walked passed her to the Managers office a few minutes later, the Manager called Emily who was asked to be his consultant, she knew this would happen even though she couldn't bare his sight and his stark grin.

"I hate my job," she thought to herself as she looked at Dwain who was seated across her in her office.

"Why this company?" she asked him,

"You have a reputation of discretion, I like my transactions discreet" Dwain answered her.

"If you are involved, I'll be needed double pay as compensation for anything strange that might happen, AGAIN." She told him stressing the "again" in her words and knowing the kind of man he was,

"I thought your company is the one that should pay you…" he suggested,

"They will but it will but for the trouble of working for you," She told him and he giggled.

Emily despised Dwain, he introduced her to drugs and when he left she used them even more, she had a special emotional attachment to him as a child and when he disappeared, she only had the drugs. After her mother died, she did not use them but later when Dwain reappeared in her life, she fell into the same hole, this time it was more intense. Dwain reappearing that time was like lost love found, in the worst way. Dwain had also lived a troubled life, he used to sell drugs in Kabwe and got in trouble with so many drug lords, after some years he went back to Lusaka to look for Emily and he found her but he had accumulated a lot of enemies because of his lifestyle so once again he abruptly disappeared from Emily's life because he put her in so much danger and left her in an even worse condition with drugs and pain. She was drown back so many times, all she wanted was to feel nothing, no pain, no love, no hatred, no anger…nothing.

If only you knew what you had put me through,
You would wipe that grin off your face and throw away those fancy
chains bought by the kind of money that almost killed me,
Almost?? Error, did kill me because I am not alive, I am dead, I
lost everything because of you, and how I wish you knew. I was so
intelligent so cheerful so energetic but you drained me.
How? You made me feel something new,
Excitement, adrenaline, momentary pleasure, I thought I had found
my treasure in smoke and packages, pills and portions
But I found the grave and there I was buried. Day in and
day out, where I went, I cannot figure out,
When I felt anger, pain and loss I was, hopeless homeless and empty,
How I tried to fill that void with anything that came my way...
Is that how you felt? Did you feel abandoned and homeless when you
lived on the streets, did the coffee and the tea make it go away?
No...I will not defend you because what you gave me, I struggled to throw away.

"Hey!" Dwain yelled, looking at Emily who suddenly bounced back to reality,
"Sign the contract," he said then she immediately signed the contract and told him to leave.

# Chapter 7

## Bundles of Joy

The next few months were difficult for both Emmy and Emily who struggled to forget the past and deal with the present, luckily they had each other and offered each other support. They were closer now more than they had ever been in their lives because they knew that they were feeling the same pain.

Laughter like little children, they were so cheerful and happy because they appreciated what they had; each other. Emmy took Emily to the supermarket to buy some groceries for her house, Emmy now had her own apartment but she visited her sister often; she preferred the lousy house with her sister than her own because she was lonely.

Emily pushed the trolley whilst Emmy stacked with things she thought Emily's house needed,

"I mean all my colleagues say I'm lucky because I have Dwain as my client, I don't see it." Emily said whilst she pushed a trolley.

"It's because you know him, come on Emily, can't you get another client…Dwain is never a good thing." Emmy told her as she put cleaning supplies in the trolley,

"Thing…haha, nicely put," Emily laughed as she dropped some vegetables into her trolley and approached the counter.

Emmy covered the cost for her sister and drove her back home. There she thought about what her sister said and began to ponder upon quitting, "What if I found a new job?" she thought to herself, "yeah, then I can apply for a job at the football association, I mean all those trophies I got during my glory days….yeah, Dwain is my last client, after which….good bye accounting hello football manager," she said loud even smiling. She felt happy, in fact she even began to clean up her house and sing and dance. When she was done cleaning she took a bath and sat in front of her TV waiting for a football match, suddenly, there was a knock at the door, she wondered who it was at that time, she shouted, "Who is it?" but there was no reply.

She assumed that it was one of the neighbours' child, so she approached the door and opened it but to her surprise it was Dwain.

"Yes?" she asked him showing that she was displeased,

"I have some transactions I need you to review." He told her putting up a charming face but he wasn't fooling her.

She grabbed the papers, quickly reviewed them and handed them back to him, "please explain, what I should tell my people?" he asked her, then she let him in and went through the documents again with more details and explained everything to him,

"You know, you could have brought this to the office," she told him,

"Well, truth is, you know, you've really helped me and the politicians I'm working for so I thought, maybe I could take you out?" he asked in a suggestive manner,

"I've already eaten," Emily told him,

"I was referring to the football match today." He said then he made his charming face again,

"It's too late, tickets are sold out," Emily said looking another direction to avoid being fooled,

"Yea, that's why I got VIP tickets, front row seats…" Dwain said pulling out tickets from his wallet the suddenly Emily stood up, rushed to her bedroom and came back with a jacket and yelled, "well hurry before the match starts!" then she ran outside and Dwain remained laughing but followed her slowly behind and caught up with her when he found her standing still and surprised,

"Is that? How did you? Is that the..? Wow" she said in amazement referring to his car then he placed his car keys in her hands and winked at her, she was breath taken, she walked slowly towards the car touching it with the tips of her fingers, it still had the factory smell of new metal and fresh paint she opened the door slowly, got in and began to ignite the engine which made a beautiful noise, she attracted the attention of all the neighbours in the flats who were piping out of their windows and when Dwain got into the car she drove of leaving a trail of dust,

"Wow…that's the latest mustang!" a little boy yelled as he watched the beautiful car disappear into busy streets of Lusaka.

She was driving as fast as she could but trying not to go over the speed limit like the good citizen. She was running late multi-tasking driving and checking her make-up in the mirror smacking her lips together and fixing her hair. She finally arrived at a hotel and quickly rushed out of her car, her car was the main reason why she was late because it was giving her problems when starting so she had to get help to start it, the car might have been looking bad but she on the other hand was looking stunning and dressed elegantly.

She rushed into the hotel quickly lifting the amber heels up the majestic staircase whilst holding on to her dress with one hand and her purse with the other, her reflection shone on the chandelier that lit up the hotel roof and where ever she went, people stared. She was directed to the VIP lounge and there she found her boss Dr Chimboni seated with an older much more successful Doctor; Dr Collins Chalomba and his wife Professor Camille Chalomba. They sat on comfortable sofas that faced the city view, the scenery was beautiful; a deep blue curtain with city lights, some stagnant some moving and the moon shone a beautiful orange that night, the hotel fountain was sparkling and massive neon lights lit different colours that were reflected on the hotel walls but none of it was as beautiful as Emmy that night.

Emmy apologized for being late and took her seat. Dr Chimboni who was previously entertaining his guests was now speechless, he could barely talk so Emmy took over the conversation. They conversed for an hour about Health care services in Zambia and how they could be improved.

"When I read about this brave young lady here serving those dying children in the war torn district in South Sudan, I was so amazed I did everything I could to locate you. That should be the drive of medical practitioners today, it should not be all about the money," Dr Chalomba said.

They had a long conversation after that and dined together.

"Thank you," Emmy said humbly

"Of course, well my wife I and had a long flight, we should be going to rest now, so tell me," he said as he pulled out his cheque book and a ball point pen, "how much will it cost to upgrade your hospital doctor?" Dr Chalomba asked Chipala. Chipala was short of words and he wanted to be modest but honest at the same time, Dr Chalomba kept waiting and when Chipala noticed that he was growing impatient he told him the amount.

"Nonsense!" Dr Chalomba exclaimed, "I'll double it!"

"Throw in an extra 300,000 pounds from my charity," his wife added. After which Emmy and Chipala saw the old couple off to their suites. Dr Chipala was a famous Doctor and chemist who travelled across the world building clinics for the poor and he also held a position with WHO, he was a role model and the pride of the African continent. He was generous enough to offer a handsome grant to Dr Chipala's rising Mwewo hospital. When they left Emmy and Chipala remained in an awkward silence but Chipala broke the silence saying, "None of this could have happened without you. You are just…"

"Thank you," Emmy interrupted.

There wasn't much more to say so she left him standing breathless and went towards her car,

"Hey, whatever I'm paying you….I'll double it," he said

"You better," she responded.

She got into her car that had seen better days but today, she had seen a good day, her bravery was acknowledged and she was not known as the sick child but a woman who was strong and brave. She smiled and suddenly all the pain was strength. Igniting it carefully she started the car and left the hotel only leaving the fumes it was releasing behind.

That was long anticipated day was finally here, how exciting was it to leave work early in order to make it to the bank and find out if it was a true, did I get a raise? Did he pay me extra? Well soon they would find out and yes, there assumptions were right. Standards of living would increase most definitely, and what was the first thing these Lusaka women would do with their money? Visit the market of course and stock their fridges first; food first! Emily was rushing across the busy market streets, it was getting late so she had to rush and buy what she needed. As she walked passed a stand she looked in the mirror and noticed she somehow had make up on, make up? She thought to herself; it couldn't be so she walked back and tried to trace her steps carefully looking for the mirror to further study, it was gone then suddenly Emmy popped up "Emily!" she yelled frightening her, it was not her reflection, it was only her twin sister. She was surprised to see Emily, "what are you doing here?" she asked. "Where else can I woman find good vegetables?" Emmy asked her speaking their local language. They then walked together and everyone stared at the beautiful twins who were buying vegetables together. They finished purchasing what they wanted after which got into Emmy's car and Emmy drove to her sisters flats.

"I need you to help me buy a car online," Emmy said,

"Oh, finally, yea you need to, finally spending that money right." Emily told her sister laughing at her.

"At least I have a car," Emmy defended herself,

"oh, I'm buying one too…see I'm an accountant, we make money, that's what we do." Emily told her,

"Hmm, that flat of yours, get someone to fix it." Emmy said making fun of Emily.

She got out of the car saying goodbye and walking towards the stairs leading to her apartment but she paused as she approached a familiar car, it was Dwain's Audi, and he got out of it when he saw her.

"Hi?" he said, "did you receive my gift?" he asked, Emmy was silent,

"I have an offer for you," Dwain told her but she knew not to listen and continued walking.

"I'm done working with you!" she said. Then he paused and had a serious look on his face, he clamped his fist tightly causing a vein to pop up; he looked frustrated, she knew what he was about to say and tried to avoid him,

"What happened to you?" he said, "we used to be a team, you used to love hanging out with me, now you despise me?" he said,

She was getting emotional, "please stop, you tore me apart, I put myself together and you did it all over again, you almost got me killed and you left me twice, I was all alone, Emmy was busy building her life and I was just....leave!" she yelled at him but the more she tried to push him away the closer he drew to her.

"Emily, Emily," he said holding her hands, "I never wanted to leave you...ever, you more than anyone should understand how difficult life is for me. I'm not like these hypocrites who have had their lives handed to them on golden trays, I grew up an orphan, lived on the streets, everything I ate, I fought for, you know that everything I do, I do to survive...I didn't complete school, I've hustled my way to the top and I have a good feeling about the people I am working for, you're the only good part of my life, don't take that away." He said gently leaving Emily speechless with tears rolling down her cheeks.

"Come," he continued, "work with me, we can be together like you know we should, we just fit Emily. I have something to show you," he said as he led Emily into his car and began to drive,

"What are you doing?" Emily asked him with an irritated face,

"Just be patient" he said,

Dwain managed to get Emily to get into his car, he wasn't the kind a person that talked much but he had special eyes that could speak a thousand words, he drove off and Emily leaned against her chair wondering where he was taking her but her mind was thinking about what he said more, they drove through the city for about half an hour till they got into the ghetto where both Emily and Dwain spent their childhood, Emily wondered what they were doing there but she did not want to ask Dwain because she knew he would not answer so she remained silent till they got to a construction area in the outskirts of the compound and he led Emily out of the car, and they climbed some sort of little hill, when they got to the top, they stood there and Emily wondered what was going on, Dwain held her closely taking her hand and placing it on the trunk of the tree where she felt some engraving, she studied it carefully.

"This is, the thing...I wrote when we were children," she said,

"You promised that we would be together always..." Dwain said, he looked at her and he spoke with his eyes, what he told her, he had told her the first time they met as children and he told it her every day from then whenever he looked at her, then he pulled out his phone and began to show Emily some blue prints.

"What's this?" Emily asked,

"My Boss, he has many projects, he assigned me to this one, it's a sports centre he's building for the community, it's meant to scout rising sports stars from ghettos and its grand, its Dope, actually that's the name I gave it. I want you to be the manager, no else can do it better than you Emily." Dwain said blowing Emily away, she was speechless. She just hugged him and sobbed whilst she did it, they shared a connection and when she hugged him, he lifted her face towards his and kissed her.

That night she felt something new, something she never really
knew. It was a sudden fear and a sudden sense of relief.
A sudden happiness and the prospect of certain pain.
Let's just say her feelings were mixed, that night as she stood at the top of a little hill the stood above the city, she felt younger again and was able to dream again of a different reality.
He lifted her up and they sat on the branch of the tree, his hands around her waist
and her head on his shoulder, looking at nothing in particular but just staring at
the city silently looking at the streets which they knew more than anyone.
She remembered the isolation she felt when she was younger, judged
and misunderstood by everyone except for Dwain.
Dwain, Dwain, Dwain what did he want this time, she knew he was bad company...
the worst kind but she tried to justify it. There was a conflict, in her heart and
mind; she did not know who to believe. What if he left again abruptly when
she did not expect it, or worse what if she got involved in his bad deals?
What if I fell in love, with the night before day came, I could hold and kiss the stars before they became invisible. At this moment, I do not feel pain but my heart leaps with joy on the inside, for a second I push all my worries away in the back of my mind to enjoy this beautiful moment that I share with you. It is like a dream come true to hear, see and feel all this, for all this time I have longed to break out of my chain and pursue what I really love and cherish.
Tell me who are you, that you understand me so well and pay a close attention to me,
to hear me out, please overcome my doubt for what I feel, are these feelings real?
Or will you do what you always do. What you always did, how you lift me so high
up and throw me to the ground, there I fall and lay on the ground alone.
But I love you, for that is the only thing that is certain, that I love you.

"What is wrong with you?"

Rage filled the room of the little house, it was a mess, everything was everywhere but mostly in boxes and plastics, someone was definitely moving out but not leaving in good terms. Emily was busy, she was walking to and fro but did not seem to know exactly what she was doing, she was being followed behind by her sister who could not stop pursuing her and raising her voice at her, there was definitely a conflict.

"What is wrong with you?" she said again, "Dwain leaves you half dead, and immediately he comes back you go racing into his arms again." She said but there was no response Emmy looked at her sister with disgust, she had never been so angry that it scared Emily who was quiet because she had nothing to say, she knew her sister was right. She tried to ignore her and continue packing since she was moving out but her sister could not stop pursing her, it started to get on her nerves.

"Emmy, leave me alone, I'm a big girl, I can make my own choices," Emily said in the kindest tone she had but Emmy yelled even the more loudly.

"Why not just keep on working at the Consultancy, you were going to find a better job later you are smarter than this," Emmy told her, she had found at about Emily's job at District Organization Promoting Exercise and Sport (D.O.P.E.S).

"Oh, later…huh, when you are married to that doctor with ten children and you take over the Health system of this country, where will I be." Emily said,

"Emily, that's not what I meant," Emmy said in a softer voice, she saw that she was not going to convince her sister so she began to walk away but before she left she said, "This time when you fall, don't expect me to catch you."

## Chapter 8

### *Blood stained eyes*

I stared at my reflection as if in a mirror…I was confused as to whether it was me or someone else. Eyes blood stained swollen with pain and veins pumping, pumping blood to heart that was failing and a body that was dying, I watched as the tears washed away all that was left, was I beholding myself? Doctors rushed into the room and nurses drugged me, I tried to comprehend what was happening around me.

A year ago,

Fireworks lit up the sky like a million shooting stars colours and sparks filled the night sky in a magnificent array forming shapes of all sports balls and finally the last firework exploded loudly like thunder leaving the Zambian flag in the sky that somewhat waved. It was finally the end of the All Africa Games and the winners were named, athletes all around had gathered in one place; they were anxious, they were tired and they were happy. The games were declared as successful by all those who participated, at the end of the closing Ceremony a special medal was to be presented by the Sports Manager to all the sponsors of the event.

"We have witnessed tremendous things here, we have seen dreams come true, we have seen talent never witnessed before but most important we have seen Unity that extends beyond borders to reach the heart of each athlete here. We have one thing in common that is our mother land and today on behalf of the motherland I would like to thank in person the ones who put this together. Now I'm pretty excited to hand awards to these honourable people, always thought it would be the other way around but…" there were laughs in the crowd, "Finance Bank…." Then there were claps as the announcements were made and the Awardees walked up to receive their medals, "finally, to the man who made our dreams come true, the one who built this stadium, the wonderful leader and friend, honourable Steven Mwansa."

Meanwhile, somewhere else there sat a man in front of his television watching the event live in his living room, he was joined by his wife who brought him a bowl of fruit salads.

"Does she want to start a political war?" he said to his wife who did not quiet seem to understand what he was saying,

"She is clearly campaigning for the opposition party, they're the ones who built that stadium years ago." He said but his wife did not comment,

"Honey, you need to talk to her," he said to his wife,

"I did, this Saturday at church," she responded,

"So is that how it is, you talk at church only?" he asked his wife, she looked at him but suddenly she felt so strange there was a sharp pain in her abdomen followed by bleeding,

"Call the ambulance," she said then she fainted.

Meanwhile at the event there were more fireworks lit and it was finally declared over although some people were heading to the after party. There were so many journalists who asked so many questions,

"Miss Lengwe, do you think Hon. Steven Mwansa is the right candidate for the next elections?" one journalist asked the woman who was being led out of the venue,

"In my opinion?" she asked the journalist,

"Well do you think he can make a just president after his court case?" another journalist asked causing her to stop walking and look at the journalist directly in his face and ask,

"Sir what's your name?"

"Iamu Zee," he responded,

"Look around you? What do you see," she asked him

"Sports, Famous people from all over the continent, development…" he responded

"Don't think about what kind of president you want, think about what kind of Zambia you need, we all need a developed Zambia," she told him leaving all the journalists with no further questions.

As she got into her car she found a thank you card, she opened it carefully as the car took off, it said 'Your work is appreciated, you can be sure to have a seat on the table.' and she smiled as she closed it and leaned back on her seat, she was exhausted, it had been a long week organising the All Africa Games and all she wanted was to lie down, suddenly she felt a strange anxiety when her phone was started ringing, it was Chipala who was calling her and she hastily picked up her phone answering it and speaking to her brother-in-law,

"Mwewo General Hospital," she said to the driver as she put her phone down. When she got there she rushed looking for Emmy who had passed out, she found Chipala standing in front of a room and she approached him.

"What happened?" she asked him,

"they are carrying out tests…I'm still waiting," Chipala told Emily, when the doctors left the room Emily and Chipala immediately went in to find out what was wrong with her.

They approached the Doctor asking so many questions.

"What's wrong?" Emily insisted,

"Don't worry, she's fine. I'm glad to say that… uhm… she's expecting." The Doctor said,

"Expecting what??" Emily asked in despair.

"I'm pregnant." Emmy said, half awake, lying down on the hospital bed.

"Oh," Emily responded, there was an awkward silence in the room for a short while until, Emily started laughing, she stayed with her sister for most of the night. This was the first time they had an honest conversation since their argument.

"Wow, sis so? A lil Emm right?" Emily said,

"Yes, so it is. I'm, I don't know, I'm excited but I'm nervous too." Emmy responded,

"Any names yet? How about naming her Emily??"

"Never!" Emmy yelled,

"Chipala will have to choose the name, he talked about naming his first Son after his grandfather,"

"I can't wait for the baby shopping? You know what, I want a kid too, I'll ask Dwain to marry me." Emily said making her sister laugh.

"You're such a dude," Emmy laughed

Emily left the hospital later that night when her sister fell asleep, she had to drive herself home since she told the driver he could go. It was late and now she was even more exhausted. She got into her car and began to drive home, on her way she received another phone call, this time it was from a strange number.

"Hello,"

"Em...emm, I need you, help..." the voice sounded broken and whoever was calling was distressed, Emily was really worried, she wondered what was wrong with the night,

"Who's this…Dwain is that you."

Immediately she made a sharp turn and headed in the opposite direction, she was so afraid and her heart was pounding. He sounded beaten up and tormented, she rushed to find him using his smartphone to track him and she found herself in a market square late at night looking for him it was dark and cold, the market was empty and she could barely see anything, she searched around for about thirteen minutes everywhere in the dirty market and she was losing hope, she searched around some vegetable stands and canteens and while she was looking she saw something near a pole flashing, it was a light from Dwain's phone and she immediately rushed to get him, he was leaning against a pole beaten up and bleeding.

"Dwain, Dwain," she said as she hurried to him, she tried to lift him up but he was too heavy, she drugged him, his injuries were serious.

"Wait here," she told him as she rushed to get her car and she parked it close to him, then she lifted him into the car and sat in the front seat shivering from fear,

"I'm gonna, I'm gonna rush you to the ER, I can call Chipala to send an ambulance," she said,

"Noo…" he whispered,

"Dwain, you need medical attention," she tried to convince him,

"The police will…" he said eating up his words. She knew then that she had to hurry to her house so that she could treat him herself.

"Who did this to you?" she asked him.

"Seven spirits…"he responded, his eyes twirling around.

When she got home she asked her guard to help her carry him in and she tended to his wounds cleaning and bandaging them, when Dwain got a little comfortable he fell asleep but Emily could not sleep, she sat on the chair waiting for him to wake up. Immediately he opened his eyes he saw her seated in front of him.

"What happened?" she asked.

"Emily, I'm still wounded," he told her and she stood up, "really," she said then she slapped him,

"What did you do!" she yelled and he started to laugh,

"Wow…I should fear you instead," he said then she lifted her hand again and threatened him till he gave in.

"I was closing a deal," he said,

"With seven spirits," she said in despair

"But he lost money and he got angry, told his boys to kill me."

"Dwain, you are already dead, you know not to…ohh," she said as she became powerless, "Dwain what have you done."

"He won't even come close, we are now riding on the clouds, trust me baby," Dwain said as the words struggled to leave his swollen lips.

Emily knew not to trust Dwain, she knew things were not going to go well, he had upset a dangerous gang leader who had a personal squad of assassins.

She knew what she had gotten herself into, at this moment there was no turning
back, she had already lost so much and had no more strength to fight.
She had made her predictions and done her calculations, there was
no way of wining, there was no way getting past this.
Her anger was like a grave within her burying all her hope
and humanity, her pain the cause of her insanity,

She tried to block it all out, she tried to carry on with her life
pretending not to know and not to see what stood before her.
Clear as sunlight.

Six months later,

Emmy's condition was unstable, doctors predicted that the closer she got to delivery, the more critical her condition would become, she was on a special treatment that made her remain strong and fit but soon she was too weak, she was lucky she had married the owner of the best hospital in the nation; she got the best treatment available but her life still hang on a thin line.

Emily walked into the door with flowers and fruits, it was a beautiful house located just behind the Hospital with a gate the driveway lead to the main road but it also had a small gate that led to the hospital both guarded by guards, Emily needed no introduction; the guards knew that she went to visit her sister. She wore a black suit with a trousers and shades covering her eyes, she walked into Emmy's room and smiled.

"Wow, you look serious," Emmy said,

"I have to, my job got very serious." Emily said,

"I heard, congrats….Minister of Sports." Emmy said,

"thanks but that's not the reason, the takeover has presented many difficulties with the previous government that need to be handled critically." Emily said,

"Sorry, are you Defence Minister?" Emmy asked teasingly.

"How are you?" Emily asked her,

"Well, the closer I get to the birth the more…difficult it becomes, but I'm not too bad," Emmy said.

"I really don't want to ask this but, what are the probabilities of both of you…making it?" Emily asked, then Emmy shed a tear and shook her head. Emily's face turned pale, she stood in front of her sister with no words to say. Emily knew what her sisters tears meant, she couldn't imagine life without her sister but this was not time to shed tears, she had to show strength to her sister.

Dwain had risen to power with the government he served, a few months ago they exposed the ruling government for major crimes and they were voted into power. It was a major symbol of democracy and the new government was supported by so many great powers but they too had so many secrets that they kept hidden.

Meanwhile in a closed door meeting a report was received that one of their enemies had escaped from prison and they came were strategizing about how to handle the situation.

"He will expose the deep dark secrets of this party if he is not found." Said the current president Steven Mwansa.

"I will find him," Dwain assured the President,

"No! you did not handle the last situation properly." Said the President, "I'll handle it."

Chipala worked so hard to ensure that his wife received everything possible, he knew how critical her condition was and he wanted to save the lives of both Emmy and his child. He was able to get the support of Dr Collins Chalomba who knew a special Chinese treatment that would help and he sent Chipala some Chinese doctors to aid her situation. When the doctors arrived they began the treatment immediately and the results were miraculous, she got back on her feet and even wanted to return to work but Chipala would never let her. The months passed by fast and soon Emmy was going to give birth, everyone was afraid because in spite of her improvements, labour was a different story.

She stood staring out of her large office windows drinking a warm cup of tea late at night, her office had medals and trophies decorating the poor government infrastructure. She pondered upon her work and a little on her life, she wore a grey stripped suit; grey trousers that enhanced her beautiful figure, a white office shirt and a grey cardigan over it, her hair covered her shoulder in a wavy shimmering pattern and she looked beautiful, but her mind was elsewhere, whilst she stared at the night lights of Lusaka city she thought to herself,

"I have finally done it," she was where she always wanted to be doing what she wanted to and even though the journey was long, she had made but was it worth? Why did she feel like something was missing? She continued to sip on her tea and then she sat down, finished off her work and wrote a report, there was a knock at the door and when she invited the person in, her secretary walked in,

"Honourable, you sister called, she said she wants to see you." She said and Emily nodded and handed her a few papers,

"Send this to the Vice President's office," she said. She lifted up her bag and walked out of the office, it was empty everyone else had gone home except for her and her secretary who was now closing the doors. She walked towards her car and put on her shades. She got into the car and drove out of the premises. She used a short cut to her sister's house, for some reason she was compelled to play an Abel Chungu playlist and meditate, she had no idea why but she did it anyway. She got to her sister's house and went towards her room where she found a nurse who was friendly to her, on the bed was Emmy who was looking tired,

"Hi…guess what?" Emmy said, "the baby's coming," she said with a smile on her face.

"Why aren't you at the hospital?" Emily asked her

"well, I wanted to have a home birth, my doctor said it's ok," she responded, "it's funny that you are a doctor too, you should know better…come on, let's go to the hospital…its right there," Emily said pointing out of the window to the giant hospital structure that stood above their wall fence.

Then suddenly the nurse rushed into the room and said,

"There are people," before she could finish talking, policewomen and men came into the room aggressively and arrested Emily for theft and fraud, she was so surprised and tried to resist them, the room was filled with nurses, guards, the policemen who were trying to arrest Emily, it was a confusing situation and the guards struggled with the police officers.

"Hey! Let me go…I'm calling the president." Emily said,

"Ms he's the one arresting you." one police officer responded with somewhat a grin,

"What??? Nooo." She yelled trying to resist them but they became violent and pinned her to the wall putting handcuffs on her, Emmy could not believe what she was seeing she was so terrified that she fell into a Pneumomediastinum. Emily was driven to the police station and Emmy to the General Hospital.

At the station Emily was immediately thrown into a cell and there she saw Dwain, he was arrested on similar charges, she yelled and demanded that she should be released and also pleaded for trial but she was surprised to see Dwain who was in a cell across her very quiet.

"Dwain, what's happening," she cried but he was silent, she yelled even louder until finally he spoke,

"'Emily, I'm sorry."

"What do you mean?"

"I drugged you into this,"

"What?"

"The first deal you helped me with, was a fraud to fraud the government and that's how Steven overthrow them, Seven spirits carried out a number of assassinations but the deal was to give him immunity and free drug trafficking, Steven wanted to change the deal, that's when I was nearly killed. Seven spirits was arrested but he went missing… he," then Emily fell down into a pool of tears, she was shivering and tormented and she did not know what to do.

When everything you build comes crushing down and everything you
fought for is not there anymore, what is worth living for? What is money
when it cannot rescue you, when it poisons you to the soul?
Is it worth gaining the world to lose your soul?"
Suddenly a shadow stood in front of them a particular figure Dwain well knew,

"Child, I took you in when the orphanage threw you away, and now you double cross me." The man said, he was dressed in a police uniform but he was clearly not a policeman, his eyes were blood shot and his head was bold with a scar running across his skull like a lining, he has thick arms and tattoos of seven demons on each side. He stood tall over Dwain's cell overshadowing him with his figure and an expression that showed no remorse like Hades, he reached for his gun and shot Dwain twice in his head, Emily was so traumatised, she feel back on the floor and could barely breathe

"Seven spirits," she said then he faced her and shot her too, some policemen came running to the scene but Seven Spirits had already fled.

# Chapter 9

## *Unseen Battles*

There was an ambulance rushed to the police station, two people were battling for their lives; Dwain was already dead. The story was all over the news about how the famous twins were both in hospital and news crews tried to get into the hospital but the hospital had tight security.

It was a cold night and the hearts of so many were frozen, doctors were doing all they could to try and save the lives of both Emmy and Emily. The hospital was so busy, all energies were focused in the ER and Maternity ward nurses were running everywhere and Doctors were sweating trying to save their kind colleague and her Prominent sister. Hours went by but nothing was certain. Chipala sat in his office there was no other place he could go, he could not believe what was happening, as a doctor he was accustomed to handling bad situations but this was too much for him; the love of his life struggled for her life and the life of his unborn child, what if he had to make a choice, his sister-in-law with a gunshot wound that was aimed perfectly for her brain, would she survive? The odds were against her to make matters worse, the load-shedding the country was facing that put a strain on the hospitals energy supply, bills became unbearable.

My heart beats like a drum, a danger song
How, o how can I be strong? Telephones ringing like thunder birds singing,
Everybody wants to know but I do not know...
Why oh why, is this happening,
I have been good not perfect but tried my best all my life. From a disadvantaged
family, I fought the most, struggled to make my grades and my parents
proud. Every good in my life seemed to turn bad somehow...
The scholarship I lost,

All those curses from jealous relatives had their sting but still I rose above
the tide and became that which no one thought I could be.
I pioneered my destiny and took charge of life at a tender age, but
life is hard even when you achieve what you hoped for.

He began to pray so much that all his nerves were swollen he wished everyone could survive but the odds were against them, he knew now more than ever that only God was in control. After five hours of waiting the only breakthrough was the operation which delivered Emmy's child, a girl who needed special medical attention immediately. Chipala was relieved but he knew the sisters still had fights to win, suddenly after reading Proverbs 16:3 he was compelled to pray for his patients all of them, he called some nurses he worshipped with and they began to pray in his office, later some cleaning staff heard them praying and joined them, then some doctors who were not working joined them and some office staff joined them, the room was so filled up that they had to move to the seminar hall and later even patients joined them praying. Doctors who were not religious thought the whole situation was insane but even they knew the stakes at hand. Whilst they were praying a pastor who was in the crowd approached Chipala whilst he was on his knees and lifted him up,

"Doctor," he said, "can you get me into their rooms."

"Hmm, why?" Chipala asked him.

"I need to pray with the patients," the pastor said, Chipala walked out of the hall leaving the others praying, and lead the pastor into the room with Emmy first where the pastor was amazingly able to talk to her even though she could only nod.

"God's love overflows from generation to generation and no matter your condition, his love never fails, only your sins can separate you from his presence but never his love. I want to pray with you that he may forgive you of all your sins and shower his love on you." The pastor said then he began to pray for Emmy, Chipala did not want to accept the reality of the events and all he could do was hope. When he finished Chipala directed him to Emily's room where even Chipala could not convince his Doctors to let them in but he managed to force their way into the room where the condition was even more critical.

"God's love overflows from generation to generation and no matter your condition, his love never fails, only your sins can separate you from his presence but never his love. I want to pray with you that he may forgive you of all your sins and shower his love on you." The pastor repeated to Emily who could not even respond but immediately he started praying she grabbed his hand,

"it's just a reflex" one doctor said, the pastor continued to pray and immediately he finished everyone in the room had a strange sensation as if something had been lifted.

'I looked and beheld my reflection as if in a mirror…I was confused as to whether it was me or someone else. Eyes blood stained swollen with pain and veins pumping, pumping blood to heart that was failing and a body that was dying, I watched as the tears washed away all that was left, was I beholding myself? Doctors rushed into the room and nurses drugged me, I tried to comprehend what was happening around me it was a whirlwind of emotions and events.

It was all confusing and dark but suddenly, I saw a light beyond all the dark clouds and I followed, I followed it and I found peace.'

# Chapter 10

## *Closing and Opening Chapters*

Life has a way of taking things away when you just start to enjoy them, all the days and time wasted become the most valuable resource when there is nothing else to hold on too. For Emmy and Emily life had so many chapters but now a new one was opened, a life without sister but she held on to the hope of seeing her again.

Emily lay peaceful in a white coffins, her face still shone with the brightness of life she always had, around her body were beautiful white and red roses that Emmy had placed there one by one for her, they gave off a wonderful scent that made the scenario almost beautiful, Emmy could not bear the sight of her dead sister but she bravely stood over her and kissed her forehead, washing her sister's face with her tears.

"She was strong and brave, many people saw her as aggressive and rude but really under that cover was a girl who's fought so hard to achieve what she believed in. That's why I named my little girl after her because I want her to he just like her, just like Emily." She said after she threw a rose in the on top of her sister's coffin.

Emmy's sickness disappeared after she had given birth to her daughter. Five years later she had another child a boy who she named Chewe.

My Dear Reflection,

Life is not book, it's not a cooked up illusion or creamed fantasy…its reality. When I stare into the mirror I see my reflection, more than that I see you, My Dear Reflection and it makes me reflect on the past, how all this started. People ask me so many questions that I fail to answer, truth is I have never had the courage to, but now I do.

I am telling the world our story and I accept whatever consequences come with it, for now I am ready, the only question is; are you ready to hear it?

$$\Omega$$

Printed in the United States
By Bookmasters